Second Chance

Firehouse Blues Series: Book 10

AE Moran

The Invisible Publishing Company

Firehouse Blues Series

Contents

Chapter 1: Duke

The firehouse alarm startles me out of my thoughts. I jump in my office chair and look up at the ceiling as the noise blares through the firehouse.

I'm deep in the middle of my latest batch of resumes from my advertisements for new staff, but I have to drop everything and go out to support the crew.

I make a few last-minute clicks on my computer, but it turns out not to make a difference. I have to stop again the minute I get out into the hall.

The crew was hanging out in the breakroom. They charge the stairs and I wait by my office door so they can go first.

They rush downstairs to their trucks and ambulances. Voice yell back and forth while they scramble into their seats and fire up the engines.

I stand back while the rescue and ladder trucks and the two ambulances pull out onto the street with their lights flashing and their sirens wailing.

I pull on my turnout jacket, but I probably won't need it. I usually only supervise the rest of the crew doing whatever they need to do to handle the call.

I never know when I might need to step in, though, so I have to take all my gear. I leave my helmet, pants, boots, and breathing apparatus off. That would be overkill for the Fire Chief unless I absolutely need it .

I'm the last one here by the time I walk around the firehouse to the parking lot, get into my support pickup, and head out to follow the crew to the scene.

I check the dispatch notes on my dashboard computer on the way. The call is a major car accident on the highway with five cars totaled and dozens more damaged.

The crew hits a massive traffic jam long before we get near the scene. Keith Brewer is driving the rescue truck. He has to drive up the shoulder while the ladder truck and the two ambulances follow single file behind him.

I stay behind them, but it doesn't take us long to figure out what the problem is.

We finally get to the scene and discover wrecked cars blocking all four lanes of traffic. They form a barricade with all the other traffic packed in behind them.

The area in front of these cars looks like a war zone or maybe some kind of natural disaster.

A big rig lies overturned on its side. It must have flipped and then skidded into the other cars. More than ten cars lie smashed to pieces right up against the rig's chassis.

Beyond the disaster zone, another twenty cars stand, sit, and lie at odd angles with different degrees of body damage.

The rest of the highway stretches away into infinity with not a single car in sight.

The Fire Department vehicles don't have any problem finding enough space to park. The crew unloads and spreads out across the area to triage all the patients.

A crowd of people from the traffic jam gather at the edge of the barricade to watch.

Another group of fifty people stands off to one side of the disaster zone. They huddle together watching the scene with huge, terrified eyes.

Some of these people hold their arms around each other. Others sob loudly. At least half of them are bleeding from some body part.

A few people sit on the ground and another six lie off to the side. They need medical attention, too.

I go over there to triage them, but on the way there, I happen to catch a glimpse of one of the passenger cars smashed against the big rig's underside.

I freeze when I see the driver's door caved in and the driver slumped over the steering wheel.

I forget all about everything else. I spin around fast, charge over there, and tear the driver's door open.

I have to yank on it a few times. Don't ask me how I get it open because it's damaged beyond repair. I should have had to use the Jaws of Life to get into the car, but I somehow manage to wrench it open.

The hinges creak and groan and the door immediately starts to close again, but I don't give a crap about that.

I lunge for the driver. It's a woman.

I pull her off the steering column and push her back in the seat so I can see her. "Naomi!!" I yell in her face. "NAOMI!!"

She doesn't respond. She's unconscious with her whole face pulverized to a bloody mass of exposed flesh torn off the bone.

The force of the collision imploded the airbag when she hit it. Blood saturates her clothes from her collarbones all the way down to her pelvis. This isn't happening.

I go over her as quickly as I can, but everything I see and touch makes me panic even more. Her bones crunch under my hands.....and then I get to her abdomen.

Her big pregnant belly doesn't feel right. I should know. I've been feeling her belly growing every day through her entire pregnancy. I can't be sitting here looking at my pregnant wife completely smashed in a car accident.

I barely glance into the back seat. My baby daughter Amelia lies in the backward-facing car seat. I can only see the round dome of her head. I can't see if she's injured, too.

She's sitting way too quietly, though, and her big, soft head lies at an angle like she might be asleep.

The sight of her sends me into another hysterical flurry of activity. I'm the only person here who can help both of them.

I keep yelling Naomi's name while I try to examine her, but just saying her name out loud sends me into a frenzy. I attack her, but there's nothing I can do for her.

I pull my head out of the car and bellow across the highway, "We need some help over here!" but none of the rest of the crew is close enough even to hear me.

The other firefighters and paramedics are all dealing with different cars and different passengers just as injured as Naomi is or maybe worse—if that's even possible.

I spin around to deal with her—like I can possibly deal with her. She needs extrication with full immobilization, but I don't even have a bandage on me right now.

I couldn't extricate her by myself, but right then, when I dive back into the car, I smell gasoline.

I don't see where it's coming from, but right at that moment, flames burst out from under the hood of the car.

The flames woof around the edges of the hood and come together in a ring right there beyond the shattered windshield.

I fly into another frantic whirlwind grabbing Naomi's seatbelt and then cutting it off. I can't take the time to immobilize her. I probably won't hurt her any more than she already is. I really don't see how her injuries can get any worse.

The flames radiate heat through the windshield and through the car body. I don't stop to check how far the fire is progressing, but I can hear it building.

I grab Naomi by the armpits and end up putting my arms around her broken body to pull her out of the car.

Her shattered spine and bones offer no resistance. Holding her feels like holding a giant bag of goo with no bones at all.

She flops in my arms when I heave her out of the seat. I drag her clear and lay her on the ground fifteen feet from the wreck.

I lean back on my knees to take one more look at her before I go back for Amelia. I become aware of the rest of the crew swarming around me.

I can't spend any more time on Naomi. Sophie McNish and Brooke Elsworth come over and start working on her. I have to back off.

Keith and Danny Brewer, Billy Cates, Caleb Watts, and Ellis Barrett head for the car. They pull their hoses over to spray down the fire.

I turn around to go get Amelia out of the car seat—and at that moment, a colossal boom obliterates the car in flames.

It detonates in my face hard enough to knock me flat on my back. The same explosion sends all the other firefighters sprawling, too.

I bounce back up just as fast and charge the car. I have to get Amelia out.

I run into a solid wall of muscle when Keith Brewer gets in my face. "Stop!" he bellows. "Don't you dare go in there!"

I struggle and even try to punch him to get him out of my way. "Get the hell off me! Get away from me! My daughter is in there!"

He's a lot stronger than I am. He grabs me and shoves me back, but he doesn't let me go to try again. "Get back, Duke! You can't help her! She's gone!"

"NO!!" I rage and try again to fight my way past him.

The other firefighters surround us and attack me to wrestle me away from the car. Danny, Theo Gough, and Carter Holt are already loading Naomi onto a backboard to transport her to the hospital.

Keith glares in my face with so much agonized fury that I really start to feel scared that he might hurt me.

He points in my face. "Get out of here, Duke!" he roars. "Go! Get in the ambulance! NOW, DUKE!!"

I don't want to listen to him. My mind and body can only think of one thing. I have to go into the fire to get Amelia out. I have to save her.

The other guys drag me away against my best efforts to break their grip. They don't let me go until they haul me all the way back to the ambulance.

The firefighters load Naomi onto the gurney and Brooke and Sophie get into the back with her.

Caleb, Ellis, George Dow, and Drew Killian force me into the front passenger seat and slam the door with me sitting helpless on the seat.

I try not to listen to Brooke and Sophie yelling back and forth while they take care of Naomi in the back of the ambulance.

Drew shoots me a pained look when he gets behind the wheel. Then he doesn't look at me again when he puts the ambulance in gear and drives off toward the hospital.

Chapter 2: Ellen

I limp across the Emergency Department and meet the ambulance crew coming from the loading dock. Vince Jaeger is already opening the ambulance's back doors.

Half a dozen patients crowd the back of the ambulance. They're all bleeding, but they stand up and get out of the ambulance on their own with no help from anyone.

Vince stands off to one side while the patients shuffle and stagger into the ED. "What do we got?" I ask him.

"More walking wounded from the car accident scene. The critical patients are all already here. We have another four loads of walking wounded. Don't even ask me how many will be self-transporting." He flashes me a wild grin. "You'll be working late tonight, sweetheart."

I try not to blush when I see him grinning at me like that. He's a really handsome guy with dark hair, dark eyes, and a muscular build.

Vince is also a really nice guy and very dedicated to his job. He keeps making it obvious that he's interested in me every time I see him.

I try to pretend not to notice. My late husband Fire Chief John Brewer had dark hair, dark eyes, and a muscular build, too, but Vince isn't John.

I can't say I wouldn't be interested in Vince under any other circumstances. I'm just not ready to start thinking about anyone like that after John's death.

I try not to smile too much that Vince is flattering me with his attention. I don't want to give him the wrong idea.

I turn away from the ambulance and head back inside. "You better get back to the scene for your next load, then. See you later."

He dives for me, grabs my arm, and holds me back. "Hey, Ellen, wait! What's going on with Naomi? Everyone on the crew is asking."

"She's still in surgery. She's been in there for two hours. We won't know anything until she comes out of it—*if* she comes out of it."

I become aware of Vince holding onto my arm. I hug all the fire crew people all the time. We're very close and Vince is no exception.

This touch feels different. He pulled me closer when he turned me around. I'm standing way too close to him—almost like he might want to kiss me.

I give my arm a very light tug to pull it out of his grasp. He realizes what he's doing at the same time and lets go immediately, but it's too late—as I didn't already know that he's interested.

"Hey!" he exclaims in an even softer voice. "Do you want to go out sometime—you know....like go out to dinner or something? I would love to take you if you can get Keith or Danny to babysit the munchkin."

I turn bright red again. Now I have no choice but to turn away. "I'm really flattered, but I don't think I'm ready for that. We're having another firehouse barbecue next weekend. I'll see you there if not before."

I try to walk away again, but he comes after me. He doesn't try to touch me again, though. Maybe he thinks he crossed a line there.

"I always see you at the barbecues," he insists. "I was hoping we could go out just the two of us—so we could spend some time by ourselves. Everyone else is always around at the barbecues."

I have to make myself turn around and face him. "I'm really flattered, Vince, but seriously. I'm not ready to go out with anyone yet. I have enough to worry about just taking care of Oakleigh by myself...."

"I could help you. You wouldn't have to take care of her by yourself. That's exactly what I'm saying."

I find myself smiling at him, but this conversation is making me too uncomfortable. "That's really sweet of you, but I'm not ready to start thinking about anyone taking John's place in my life—and I don't think Oakleigh is ready for that, either. I'm flattered that you think of me that way, but I'm not ready to move on yet. Maybe ask me later....."

"Like when?" he asks. "How long should I wait before I ask again?"

"I don't know. I couldn't even begin to speculate. I better go."

I walk back into the ED and leave him and the ambulance on the loading dock. I'm supposed to be at work treating and triaging patients, not standing around flirting with a hot firefighter.

I try to shake those thoughts out of my head.

"Hey!" he calls after me. "Find out what's going on with Naomi!"

I nod and wave before I walk back inside. I can't think about him anymore. I don't want to think about him. I don't want to think about dating anyone but John and he isn't here.

I wish like anything he was here. It still hurts to go home to that house and realize he isn't here—and then I have to deal with Oakleigh.

She makes it a thousand times worse because she's so depressed and upset about his death. Time does nothing to heal that wound.

She used to be such a sweet, innocent, fun-loving kid. Now she's gloomy, moody, belligerent, and explosive. She flies off the handle over every little thing. She lashes out at the people who care about her the most.

It's interesting that the people who care about her the most, the people she lashes out at the most, are the same people who have lost the most from John's death.

Keith, Danny, and I are primarily responsible for taking care of Oakleigh. The three of us are the most grief-stricken over John's loss and we're the ones who come under fire from her when she does lash out.

I don't know if she even realizes how much worse she's making this nightmare for all of us—or maybe she does realize.

Maybe that's why she does it. Maybe she understands that the three of us care about her as much as we do precisely because we share that pain with her.

I wouldn't be surprised if that was the reason. I wouldn't be surprised if she lashes out more harshly at us because she knows she can. She already understands that we see why she's doing it and we actually love her for it.

I wish I could find a way to help her, but I can't. I can't even help myself get through it.

I can only get through it by doing my job and staying busy. I go through the Emergency Department waiting room triaging patients, stitching up lacerations, and repeating the usual round of questions to give instructions to people with concussions.

I don't see any of the ambulance crews again until hours later when Keith, Danny, Caleb, and Billy come to find me.

"What's happening with Naomi?" Keith asks.

"I don't know. I've been stuck down here all day. I haven't been able to go upstairs to find out."

"Could you find out, please?" Danny asks. "The whole crew is waiting at the firehouse. No one knows if they should come over here to support Duke or not."

"I'll find out. You can come upstairs if you want to. Then I can let you know and you can pass the word to the crew."

We get into an elevator and exit on the surgical floor. Naomi is already down in ICU, so the guys accompany me down there.

They wait out in the hall while I go into the unit to find out about Naomi. I read her chart at the nurses' station and then go take a look into her room.

She lies on the bed with her face slashed to pieces. The surgical team has stitched up the major lacerations, but the swelling makes her face completely unrecognizable. She looks like a monster—or she would if she wasn't lying unconscious in a hospital bed.

An ET tube goes into her mouth to ventilate her lungs. Another tube goes into her mouth and an IV hangs by her bed to drip fluids into her arm.

All the wires and electrodes run away from the bed to the equipment standing nearby.

The surgical team also put a shunt into her skull to relieve bleeding and pressure. It drains from the side of her head into a thick bandage wrapped around her skull.

I can't see any of the rest of her through her hospital gown and the sheets and blankets covering her, but her chart says it all.

The impact of the truck running into her car completely obliterated all the bones on the front side of her body. She has a shattered pelvis, a shattered sternum, multiple shattered ribs, two broken arms, two broken femurs, and multiple spinal fractures.

Her unborn baby didn't survive the impact. The blow of her body striking the steering column crushed the baby completely. The surgical team had to give Naomi a full hysterectomy just to save her life. Now she's in a coma and might not come out of it.

The sight of her would be bad enough, but it's the man sitting in the chair across the room that really gets my attention.

Three chairs sit against the back wall of the room. Fire Chief Duke Broebeck sits in the center chair resting his elbows on his knees.

He rubs his hands together again and again in nervous agitation. His shoulders, back, and arms tense with his movements. He looks like he wants to jump up and do something—anything to help bring his wife and unborn baby back.

Nothing will bring them back. Naomi's condition is listed as grave. The doctors must have been trying to spare Duke's feelings when they listed her condition as that. I would call it dire or even hopeless, but I'm not her doctor.

I step into the room and sit down in the chair next to Duke. He doesn't even see me.

The nervous energy coming from him immediately makes me nervous, too. The guy can't calm down to save his life.

I want to touch him....or put my arm around him.....or do something....

I don't dare to touch him, though.

The first thing that comes to my mind is to ask if he's okay, but I at least have the presence of mind not to ask that. He might attack me if I did.

"The fire crew is all supporting you," I tell him. "They're all waiting to hear the news and support you in any way they can."

He doesn't respond. He just stares at Naomi and keeps rubbing his hands together. He can't sit still. That motion moves him back and forth in his seat.

He's a powerful man of forty-five with salt-and-pepper grey hair. Just sitting this close to him feels dangerous. He could jump up at any time and then nothing would stop him from doing anything.

I also don't ask if he wants the crew to come and support him. He won't appreciate that. I'll just have to tell Keith and the others to leave Duke alone for now.

Keith will take over the firehouse until Duke goes back to work—whenever that turns out to be. The rest of the crew will keep running things in Duke's absence.

They won't stop caring, though. They'll all wait until Duke needs them to do something. That's the fire crew's superpower. They stick by each other.

Right now, he needs them to keep the wheels turning when he isn't there to do it for them. He doesn't have to worry about Howe Firehouse running itself without him.

I can't leave him alone—not after this.

He might not even realize I'm here, but I have to do something.

I lay my hand on his shoulder. I don't expect it to do any good, but someone has to be here for him. I can't let him go through this alone. "Can I do anything for you? Is there anything you need? I could take you down to the cafeteria....or take you home....anything."

He suddenly stops fidgeting when I touch his shoulder. He freezes and then, without warning, he breaks down crying his heart out. He buries his face in his hands and crumbles right in front of me.

"Amelia's gone!" he wails. "Amelia's gone! She was in the car...and now she's gone!"

Tears come to my eyes listening to him. God, what a nightmare!

He and Naomi gave everything to take care of Amelia. They gave her such a loving home—a home she never would have had without them.

Her life would have been a trainwreck without them—and now it's over because she's dead.

I put my arms around him, but he doesn't notice that, either. His whole body shakes with sobs. He doesn't sink into my embrace at all.

I wind up putting my head on his shoulder and then stroking my fingers through his hair. Nothing can comfort him from this.

His wife is in a coma and probably won't come out of it. His unborn child is dead and so is his baby daughter.

Don't ask me how Duke is even still alive under such a devastating blow as this. How can he even stand it?

I hold him for a long time while he cries. He sounds so pathetic and heartbroken. Who wouldn't be?

I wish I could do something for him, but no one can. Nothing will be able to undo this.

He cries for a long, long time, but at least he's letting it out. All that nervous energy comes pouring out through his tears.

He cries for more than Amelia. He cries for Naomi, for their unborn child, and for all the children they ever could have had if she recovers.

Their family meant so much to them. Now those dreams lie broken and dead in that hospital bed over there. How does a man survive that?

I stay with him, pet his hair, and squeeze him around the shoulders. That doesn't help, either, but at least he knows he isn't alone. That's the only thing I can do for him.

I'm still sitting there when he finally stops crying, sniffs, runs his red, raw face across the shoulder of his T-shirt, and straightens up.

He scowls across the room at Naomi....and that's it.

I take my hand down and don't touch him again. He doesn't acknowledge my presence or say anything to me—not even once.

He just goes back to sitting there in silence. He doesn't fidget or squirm in his seat or rub his hands together. All that nervous energy drains out of him. It doesn't come back.

He sits slumped and broken in his chair just staring at his injured wife. Jesus, he looks awful!

I don't want to leave him alone, but I can't stay here. I have to go home and deal with Oakleigh and all the rest of my own problems.

I stand up, rest my hand on his shoulder again, and then, just because, I kiss him on the head and stroke his hair one last time. "I gotta go, but I'll come back and check on you soon. We're all waiting to hear from you if you need anything from any of us."

I kiss him on the head one more time and walk out of the room. I have to leave sometime. I need to get it over with soon before I get stuck here.

He'll keep sitting here holding this silent vigil to a life that no longer exists. His life no longer exists. The poor guy.

I head out of the ICU and find Keith, Danny, Billy, and Caleb pacing around in the waiting room. They all rush me when I come out.

"What's going on?" Keith glances behind me. "Where's Duke? Is he okay?"

"No, he isn't. He's a mess—as you can expect. I don't think you visiting him is a good idea—not yet."

"How's Naomi?" Caleb asked.

"Not good. She's in a coma—and she lost the baby. The collision completely pulverized the baby and ruptured her uterus. The surgical team had to give her a hysterectomy to stop the bleeding."

Keith hisses through his teeth and jerks his head away. "Man! That is rough!"

"Yeah," I murmur. "Duke is pretty much gone. I couldn't even begin to guess when he'll come out of it. You better take over the firehouse."

"Of course," Keith snaps. "Tell him he doesn't have to worry about any of that. We'll handle everything."

I smile at him—at all of them. "I won't tell him because he wouldn't even hear me. He's too buried in his grief right now—but I'm sure he already knows he can count on all of you."

"Damn," Danny murmurs. "Poor guy."

"Yeah," I reply. "That doesn't even begin to cover it. You guys should get out of here. That's what I'm going to do. He won't want us hanging around. We all know what we need to do, so we'll just have to keep doing it the way we did when we lost John. Duke needs to know that we'll keep going no matter what. I'm sure he appreciates the fact that we all care about him and Naomi so much."

Keith squares his shoulders at me. "Of course. Thank you, sweetheart. We'll go." He steps forward to hug me. "Call us the minute anything changes."

"I will." I hug the other three and they leave. Now it's my turn to go out there and face reality.

Chapter 3: Ellen

I yell up the hall to the other end of the house. "Oakleigh! Breakfast time! Hurry up or you'll be late for school!"

She yells back in a furious roar. "I'm coming! You don't have to yell at me!"

I groan and roll my eyes to Heaven. Here we go again. We go through the same old routine every morning—or any other time I try to tell her what to do.

I turn back to the stove and serve our scrambled eggs onto two plates, one for her and one for me. I put them both on the table by the time she comes storming in from her bedroom.

She throws herself down in the chair and starts stabbing her fork into the eggs. "Why do I have to go to school at all? Why can't I home-school?"

"We've already talked about this. I don't think that would be a good idea when you're already isolated. Besides, I have to work. You couldn't stay home by yourself."

"What about today? You have the day off."

I sit down across the corner of the table and make a face at her. "Please. Are you really ready to make me a solemn promise on your sacred word of honor that you'll spend the day doing schoolwork—or will you just mooch around in your room doing whatever you feel like?"

She looks away. Of course. This whole home-school argument is nothing but a ploy so she doesn't have to deal with the world.

She's been on my case ever since John died to let her isolate herself even more than she already is. I wouldn't be doing my job as her guardian if I let her completely cut herself off from the human race—which is exactly what she seems to be trying to do.

I take a few bites of my eggs and get up the get myself a cup of coffee when I hear a car door slam outside. I glance through the window.

"That's strange," I murmur. "Keith and Danny are here."

Her head shoots up. "What for? It's first thing in the morning."

"I don't know, but it must be something important." I open the front door just as Keith and Danny climb up on the porch in front of me. "Hey! What's going on? This is a surprise."

Keith waves a file folder at me. "We need to talk to you about John's estate. Some legal wrinkles have come up with his will and the custody arrangements between you and Oakleigh."

"Come on in." I wave both of them inside. "Take a seat. We were just having breakfast."

Keith and Danny approach the table. They both do their best to smile at Oakleigh, but things haven't been as warm between the three of them as they once were.

"Hey, sweetheart," Keith greets her.

"What is this about Dad's will?" she demands. "I'm not moving away from Ellen. I'm staying here with her."

"We already know that," Danny replies. "That isn't why we're here."

"Why *are* you here?" she fires back.

"That's between me and the boys," I tell her. "Finish eating and get ready for school while we handle this."

She doesn't finish eating before she storms off to her room in a huff. She even slams the door extra hard.

I heave an almighty sigh and pass my hand across my eyes. "Sorry about that. Take a seat. She'll be leaving for school in a minute. Then we can talk."

Keith pulls out a chair. "It isn't a big deal. We can work this out in a few seconds. We just need to close this loophole in John's will."

"What's the problem? John made me Oakleigh's legal guardian. I thought we all agreed on that."

"We did—and he did," Danny replies. "For some reason, the lawyer who handled probate on the will thinks there was something wrong with the wording of the custody clause. He says the stipulation of guardianship isn't valid—which means custody would fall to me and Keith—not you."

Oakleigh comes back just in time to hear the last of his statement.

"I told you I'm not moving away from Ellen!" she shrieks before anyone can say another word. "I don't care what you do! You are NOT taking me away! I hate you! I never want to see you again! Don't you dare take me away from Ellen!"

"No one is taking you away from anyone," Keith tells her. "This is just a legal mix-up….."

"You said you were going to take custody of me!" she bellows. "I'll never let you take me! I'll run away! You have no right! You're all against me! I hate you!"

She snatches her backpack and lunchbox, blasts through the front door, and takes off running down the block.

I have to go over there to shut the door because she leaves it hanging open.

Then I wilt into my chair. "Sorry about that."

"Stop saying that," Danny tells me. "This isn't your fault. You're a blinkin' hero for putting up with her as long as you have. I couldn't do it."

I groan in agony. "I don't know how much more of this I can take. She's so touchy. She flies off the handle even if I just tell her to come for breakfast. She's impossible."

"What do you want us to do?" Keith asks.

"What *can* we do?" Danny asks. "She clearly doesn't want to come live with either of us."

"I honestly don't think it makes any difference who she lives with," I tell them. "I don't think this has anything to do with you or me—but we already know that." I sigh and turn back to Keith. "So what are we doing about this custody thing?"

"The legal beagles are already rooting around in their law libraries trying to straighten out the language of the will."

"But they can't change the language of the will," I point out. "John's already dead. You can't rewrite a will after the person dies."

"I know. What I meant was that the legal beagles are trying to straighten out an addendum to the will that actually, legally assigns custody to you instead of us."

"The problem is that John changed the will after you two got together," Danny tells me. "Everything else about the will is exactly the same way it was before you moved in here. The lawyers think the language makes the most recent will invalid, which means the last valid will takes effect—which is the will that assigned legal guardianship to me and Keith."

I throw up my hands. "I really don't have the brain cells to understand this right now. Are you telling me the lawyers are already working on straightening this out? Do I need to do anything or sign anything?"

"Not yet," Danny tells me. "They plan to draw up a new document that makes you Oakleigh's legal guardian along with us. All three of us will have equal custody decision-making power over her." He looks up at me. "I hope you're okay with that."

"Of course! One hundred percent. That sounds perfect."

"That way, one of us could take over if our circumstances change," Keith explains. "Oakleigh might decide she hates you instead of us and that she doesn't hate us as much as she thought she did. Then she could come to live with one of us with no interruption in services."

I snort. "Be careful what you wish for."

"What I mean is, if it happened and she did come to live with one of us—or if something happened to you—we wouldn't have to go through this whole legal song and dance all over again. Whichever one of us took her would already have full custody and legal guardianship."

"She'll keep living with you until the lawyers finish drawing up the paperwork," Danny tells me. "As long as you're okay with that."

I try to smile at both of them, but my heart isn't in it. "Sometimes I wonder if I'm the best person for her."

"What are you talking about?!" Keith fires back. "Of course you are! Who else would she stay with? You just heard her. She doesn't want to live with anyone else. You're the one person who understands her."

"Maybe that's the problem. Maybe the two of us living together is just keeping both of us locked in a cycle of grief and pain with no way to get out of it. Maybe the two of us living together is just two injured hearts rubbing against each other making each other bleed."

"She would have the same problem with either of us," Danny points out. "We're both hurting just as much."

"But at least she wouldn't be stuck alone with me. You have Zeke, Emily, and the baby. Keith has Leila and Leon. She would at least be part of a family if she went with you. She would have no choice but to face reality instead of staying locked in her own little dark bubble."

"Being part of a family could make it worse for her," Keith points out. "She might see all of us living our lives and moving on and she might feel abandoned and ignored. She might resent us and think we were forgetting John."

Tears spring to my eyes before I have time to stop them. "Well, I'm trying to forget John, too, you know! Maybe it isn't best for me to keep living with the one person who keeps me locked in the past!"

Keith gets out of his chair in a heartbeat, comes over to me, and puts his arms around me. "Okay," he breathes. "I know. If you want us to take her, we can."

"I don't!" I wail. "I don't want her to leave! I just don't know what to do with her! I'm not even her mother!"

"You're the next best thing for her." Keith kisses me on top of the head. "Even John knew that or he wouldn't have left you in charge of her."

He steps back and I see Danny wiping tears off his cheeks. I love these guys more than anything. At least I'm not the only emotional wreck around here.

Keith kisses me on the forehead this time. "You're doing a great job with her. You just keep doing exactly what you're doing—and if you need a break, all you have to do is tell us. We'll take her off your hands. So what if she hates us? So we'll start the adolescent years early. No problem."

I try to laugh, but I only wind up sobbing again. Keith pulls me into another hug. I can cry on his shoulder because I know that he and Danny are going through the same thing.

I finally pull myself together enough to straighten up. Keith won't stop rubbing my arms and stroking my hair. He's so big and kind. Both he and Danny are the salt of the Earth—just like John.

I can't let myself start thinking that or I'll start crying all over again. I miss John like anything. Every day is a torture.

I just have to keep going.

I force myself to turn away, get a tissue from the box on the living room coffee table, and face life with my head up. "Sorry about that."

"Stop it," Danny tells me.

I blow my nose and glare at Keith's file folder. "So it's all taking care of itself, right?"

"Right," Keith tells me. "You don't have to do anything except keep on taking care of her. We'll handle the legal stuff."

"Thanks....for everything."

He kisses me on the temple again. "We'll get out of your hair." He starts to turn away and changes his mind. "Oh, one more thing. We need to talk to you about the barbecue."

"What about it? It's this Saturday."

"I know....at least, I know you and Leila planned for it to be this Saturday."

I frown at him. "What do you mean—we planned for it to be this Saturday? It still is."

"Are you sure?" he asks. "What about Duke....and Naomi?"

I open my mouth to answer and stop myself. "Oh. Right. I didn't think of that."

"None of us can decide if we should go ahead with the barbecue considering everything that's happening," Danny interjects. "We don't want to disrespect what Duke is going through....but we don't want to cancel the barbecue, either, unless we have to."

"Where is he?" I ask. "Where is Duke?"

"No one knows," Danny replies. "None of us has dared to go back to the hospital since you told us not to. We don't know what's going on with Duke or Naomi."

"We were hoping you could tell us—and tell us what to do about the barbecue," Keith goes on.

"Me?!" I counter. "I'm not even part of the firehouse crew. I'm not even technically connected to the firehouse anymore."

"Oh, come on, sweetheart!" Danny chides. "You'll always be part of the firehouse until the day you die. You didn't actually think John's death changed that, did you? You practically run the barbecues. We couldn't keep having them at all without you."

Now it's my turn to snort. "Please. I'm sure any of the others would be perfectly capable of organizing a friendly barbecue at the beach. Are you really telling me Carter Holt couldn't organize a barbecue? Don't make me laugh."

Both of them do laugh. "Okay, you got me," Danny replies. "But you were the one who organized this one. Do you think we should cancel it or not? It seems so inappropriate to go ahead with it when Duke and Naomi are going through this nightmare."

"We thought it would be inappropriate to have barbecues after John's death, but we went ahead with them then and it was the right thing to do," I point out. "Maybe we should go ahead with these, too."

"But John wasn't around to tell us one way or the other," Keith counters. "Duke is still around. We don't want to offend him or make him think we don't care enough about what he's going through."

"We need to ask him," Danny suggests. "You should ask him, Ellen."

"I can't ask him! I don't even work for the guy."

"That's why it has to be you," Keith tells me. "You're the only person involved who doesn't work for him, so technically, you're the only person who *can* ask him."

"I don't know about that."

"Come on, sweetie," Danny tells me. "Take one for your old crew."

I find myself smiling at both of them. "Fine. Be that way. I'll do it and tell you what he says."

"Thank you so much." Keith dives in and kisses me on the cheek. "We're only a phone call away if you or Oakleigh need anything."

Chapter 4: Duke

I'm just trying to straighten out my eyeballs to read the fourteenth resume for the open paramedic position when someone knocks on my office door.

"Come in!" I call.

The door opens. I stare in a moment of confusion when Ellen Foreman limps into my office.

"Hello," I tell her. "What are you doing here?"

She hobbles to my desk, sits down in one of the chairs, and unlocks the knee joint of her leg brace so she can bend her leg.

"I've been looking for you," she tells me. "I thought you would be at the hospital, but you obviously weren't there. I'm surprised you're here considering everything."

I have to look away. I concentrate on my computer instead. "I was going crazy there. I had to get out. This place takes my mind off it—and none of the doctors can tell me when Naomi might come out of her coma anyway. I have no reason to stand around waiting. They'll call me if her condition changes."

She winces. "I assume you mean her condition hasn't changed."

"Didn't you check? Didn't you see her chart—while you were looking for me?"

A trace of a very sad smile touches the corners of her lips. "I didn't look at her chart. I was worried about you, especially when I realized you were here."

I look away again. I don't want her worrying about me.

I can't explain why, but her attention makes me uncomfortable—and not because my wife is in a coma—or because I just lost my baby daughter and my unborn child in a car wreck.

Everyone around here already knows all of that, but I find it somehow so much harder to face Ellen with that truth hanging over my head.

I don't even care that she saw me at my lowest point in the hospital. I actually appreciate that she was there—and that she was the one who triggered it so I could actually get my feelings out.

Ellen is awesome. Everyone at the firehouse loves her and for good reason. I have nothing but admiration and affection for her, especially because of what she did for me at the hospital.

None of that bothers me—but it somehow brings us closer. It brings us closer in a way that I don't want to be close with someone right now.

I don't want to be close with anyone but Naomi. I don't want someone else supporting me or even caring about me.

If they did, I would have to face the fact that I actually have something that needs to be supported and cared for.

I just want to distance myself from all of this. I was doing that just fine before Ellen walked into my office. Now I can't escape it. She embodies it. She's a living, breathing reminder that I'm not okay at all

She changes the subject in her usual smooth, easy, comfortable way. She looks around the office at everything. "Wow. I never thought I would ever set foot in this office again."

"It must be a special occasion if you came all the way down here." I lean back in my chair. "What can I do for you?"

She scans the walls. My certifications hang there where John Brewer's used to hang.

She only looks for a second before she comes back to facing me. "The crew wants to know how you feel about us going ahead with this weekend's barbecue. No one feels right about going ahead with it, considering what you and Naomi are going through."

I feel my hackles start to rise. "Couldn't one of the crew just come out and ask me that? Why did they elect you as their representative?"

"Maybe because none of them wants to upset you or offend you. Maybe because they're all tiptoeing around you like a simmering volcano ready to explode. Anyway, I'm the only person involved with organizing the barbecue who doesn't work for you—so you can't fire me if I do offend you."

She bursts into a huge grin. It lights up her face and makes her even more hauntingly warm and appealing than she usually is.

I don't know how anyone can grin like that after just losing their spouse the way she did. I couldn't grin like that—not now. I don't know if I'll ever be able to smile again as long as I live.

She just keeps going, though. She lost the one most important person in her life—and now she's raising his daughter in his place.

Ellen never stops. She just keeps doing the job, taking care of patients, and being a goddamn rock for the rest of the firehouse crew.

She's an inspiration. I couldn't get offended by her even if I wanted to.

I can't hold eye contact with her, though—not when she knows how raw and fragile I am right now.

She's the one person I can't hide it from. Work just covers it up, but she can still see it. She'll always be able to see no matter what I do to cover it up.

I try to face my computer again, fail, and wind up mumbling under my breath. "You should all have the barbecue without me. I won't go. I would only make everyone uncomfortable."

"We don't want to have it without you," she tells me. "No one feels like celebrating any more than you do."

"No, you should," I say way too quickly. "You should enjoy yourselves."

"We want to support you. We're family. None of us wants to think about moving on when you're hanging in the balance."

"I appreciate that, but I don't need any support. You should do it even if I'm not there. In fact, I won't be there. I would only bring everyone down."

She studies me way too closely across the desk, but she doesn't try with me or even try to talk sense into me.

She stands up and locks her knee joint so she can balance on her brace. She does it effortlessly and with perfect fluid grace. She stands up at the same speed as any other person.

"Okay, we'll go ahead with it," she tells me. "You're more than welcome to come if you change your mind. You won't bring us down or anything. It might make you feel better to take some time off with people who understand what you're going through. We all want to be there for you if you'll let us."

I look away again. I can only mumble, "Thanks."

"Don't work too hard, okay? You have my number if you need anything."

She walks out and I try to get back to work, but her visit disturbs me more than if someone else on the crew interrupted me.

Her care and interest in my situation means the world. She's right. I probably would have gotten defensive and bitten back if one of the crew tried to talk to me about attending a social event like the barbecue.

I would have considered it an insult when I don't know if Naomi will live or die.

Ellen is the only person who could have come to talk to me about it.

I get a rush of grateful relief that someone is interested enough to check on me—someone other than the crew.

I know they aren't worried about how well I'm running the firehouse. That isn't the reason they don't come to check on me. They care about me just as much, but it means something different when she does it.

Part of me really wishes I could sit somewhere with her, somewhere alone and quiet, and pour out all the bitter anguish and bruised fury in my soul.

Part of me wishes like anything I could break down sobbing on her shoulder. She's the only person disconnected enough from the firehouse who would be able to be there for me that way.

She would understand. She would be able to accept my feelings without judgment. She wouldn't think less of me for being in pain over all of this.

I know the firehouse crew would accept it, too, but I wouldn't be able to express it to them. I'm their boss.

I turn back to my computer for the dozenth time, but I can't stop thinking about her visit. I probably won't go to the barbecue.

I don't feel like celebrating, either—not that the barbecue would be any kind of celebration. I just can't stop working even for a second. I might start thinking too much if I do.

It sure is nice to know that she cares, though. It's nice to know I have someone on the outside that I can turn to if I want to. That means everything.

Chapter 5: Ellen

I open the door of my car, swing my legs outside, and push myself out of the driver's seat. I bend down to lock my knee brace so I can walk.

Before I can do anything, Oakleigh bursts out of the back, slams the rear passenger door extra hard, and storms off into the dunes the way she always does.

I heave a colossal sigh, but I don't try to go after her. I know better by now.

I limp around the car and open the trunk to take my bags out just as a bright red pickup truck rolls in. Vince gets out and grins at me. "Do you need a knight in shining armor? Don't worry. I have arrived."

I find myself laughing at him. "Thanks. I was just about to call the knights-in-shining-armor hotline."

He smirks and lifts my bags out of the back. "You go ahead down there and hold court with your faithful subjects. I'll get these."

I try to stop myself from blushing, but fortunately for me, Chris Daniels pulls up in her car right then. Then the whole fire crew shows up in the trucks and ambulances.

Everyone unloads talking at once. Vince gets lost in the crowd—not that I don't like the guy. I just wish he would stop hitting on me after I already told him I wasn't ready for anything.

Chris falls in at my side and takes another two bags out of my trunk. I have nothing to do now but walk down to the barbecue.

Chris squints into the dunes. "How's the bundle of joy?"

I snort. "She isn't joyful—and she doesn't bring joy to those around her, either."

"At least she's here. She needs to be around people who care about her."

"Oh, she doesn't want to be here. She won't stop nagging me to let her stay home from the barbecues. She doesn't want to come. She doesn't want to be around anyone, but I told her she has to come because she isn't old enough to stay home alone. Keith, Danny, and everyone else who would be able to take care of her are already here. If they took care of her in my place, they would only wind up bringing her here, too."

"Wow, that's terrible."

"Oh, that's nothing. She keeps pestering me to let her stay home from school and start home-schooling. She wants to isolate herself completely. I told her I don't think that's a good idea. She still needs to be around people—but her teachers say she isn't bringing sunshine and rainbows to school with her every day, either."

Chris bursts out laughing. "Pity. I guess it's understandable."

I sigh again for the millionth time. "I can only hope she grows out of it by the time she's thirty-five or so."

We laugh about it, but by that time, we make it down to the bar-becue. Everyone puts their food on the picnic table. Keith and Danny run the grill as always.

I get swept into the circle of friends standing around talking. "I heard the driver of the big rig that caused that major accident got arrested for drunk driving," Billy tells us. "He was completely blotto. He was so drunk that, when they took him into court the next day, the judge wouldn't accept his plea because the guy was still technically over the legal blood alcohol limit."

"Wow," I exclaim. "That is really bad."

"He already has more than ten counts of vehicular homicide against him and most of the other surviving patients are still in the hospital," Brooke adds. "If they go down, he'll be facing charges for them, too."

"At least he only has to go through one trial for all of them," Josh Abbott points out. "The one incident killed and injured all of the patients."

Sophie turns to me. "What's the news on Naomi?"

"No news. There's no change. She's still in ICU."

"Is there any way to know if she'll ever come out of the coma?" Caleb asks.

"The doctors aren't very hopeful based on her EEG activity and the extent of traumatic brain injury. They have to wait a little longer for all the swelling to go down. They'll remove the shunt before they decide whether they should take her off the ventilators."

"Damn," Billy mutters. "That has to be hard on Duke."

"No one will even have the conversation with him—not this soon," I go on. "He already knows it doesn't look good. They want to be sure there really is no hope before they bring it up—and they don't even know if she'll survive that long. All her other injuries are way too serious. She's barely holding on as it is."

"Poor guy," Carter murmurs. "I wish we could do something for him."

"He won't stop working," Chris murmurs. "He haunts the firehouse like some kind of crazed madman and he still attends every single call. He stays later and comes earlier than any of us. I wish we could get him to ease off."

"When I talked to him, he said work was the one thing that helped him deal with it," I tell her. "If you really want to do something for him, just let him do his job."

"We are," Josh replies. "It just hurts to see him suffering like this."

"We can't do anything about that. It's enough that he knows we all understand and care about him. Just let him cope with it in his own way. At least he can still function. He wants to keep contributing to the fire crew. It's the one thing keeping him going."

Brooke gasps and whispers in a terrified undertone. "He's here! He just pulled into the driveway! Oh, my gosh! What should we do?"

I turn around and spot Duke getting out of his support pickup. He's still wearing his Fire Department uniform. He must have just come from the firehouse.

The sight of him twists my guts. No one else on the crew says a word. All conversation dies.

"You should go talk to him, Ellen," Danny murmurs. "Invite him to join us."

"I already did," I counter. "He knows he's welcome."

"Just go talk to him," Keith insists. "Go on."

I turn away and lurch across the sand to the parking lot. I seem to be the new go-between for the crew to communicate with their own Chief.

I should resent this, but I can't. I just feel too bad for Duke.

He looks up when I get to the parking lot and immediately looks away. He fiddles with something in one of the storage compartments on the back of his truck. "Hi," he mumbles.

"Hey!" I greet him. "It's so great that you made it. We're all happy you're here."

"I'm not," he mumbles without looking at me. "Maybe this wasn't a good idea."

"Just give it a try. You don't want to be by yourself right now. Come on! Everyone is waiting for you."

He squints down the beach. "Maybe I shouldn't."

"Yes, you should. You're already here. You must have wanted to come or you would still be in your office with your face glued to your computer. Now come on. You can't back out now."

I step forward, take his arm, and pretend to tow him toward the barbecue. "I don't even know why I'm here," he mutters.

"It doesn't matter why. You need us and we want to be here for you. Everyone wants to support you and help you deal with this—the same way we all helped each other deal with John's death. Come on. These people are your family. You know that."

He doesn't say anything else nor will he look at me or anyone else when I lead him back to the circle.

Keith and Danny keep going back and forth to the barbecue. The others try their best to restart the conversation, now that Duke is here.

No one talks about Naomi's condition or the wreck that put her in the hospital.

"What are you drinking?" Josh asks Duke. "We have iced tea, soda, and some kind of mushroom stump water brew that Jessie brought."

"Hey!" Jessie Nash counters. "It isn't mushroom stump water brew! It's kombucha! It's very healthy and it tastes great."

"We aren't here to be healthy. We're here to dose ourselves with enough sugar to put a diabetic in the morgue." Billy takes one of the sodas out of a cooler and passes it to Duke. "Here. Drink this."

Duke tries unsuccessfully to smile and murmurs low, "Thanks."

"Are any of the new resumes looking promising?" Carter asks.

"A few of them. I already scrapped half of them for past criminal activity or because the applicants got fired for personality problems at their old jobs."

"Half?!" Keith throws up his hands. "Jesus! That's it! Take me off the Fire Chief training course right now! I can't face that!"

Duke chuckles once and stops himself. "It isn't all it's cracked up to be. Maybe I should make you hire the new people."

"How many positions are you trying to fill?" I ask.

He barely glances at me. "I'm going to hire as many qualified people as I can get. We need a few more than we have open positions."

"Why do we need more?" Caleb asks. "Don't you have a limited budget for staff salaries?"

"Budget?" Duke counters. "You want to talk about the budget for staff salaries? Let's talk about all the overtime you people have been logging to cover our unmanned shifts. Let's talk about all the overdue vacation days and sick time I'm going to have to cover just as soon as I find the people to do it. I'm going to need a lot of extra people for that. I don't even know if I have enough qualified people in this stack of resumes to do all that."

Another hushed silence falls over the group. "I didn't think of that," Sophie murmurs. "You're right. None of us has been able to take time off since Ellen got hurt."

"What about Theo going on vacation?" Jessie asks. "You asked Ellis to cover Theo's shifts so he could take his sick days off."

"I had to call him back early," Duke replies. "We were too short-handed even then."

I bump his elbow. "Do you want something to eat? I can get you a plate."

"Thanks," he mumbles. "I'm really grateful to all of you for your support."

"Forget it, man." Keith waves toward the grill. "Come over here to the barbecue and tell me which dead animal you want to dismember for your lunch."

Keith takes Duke to the barbecue. I go over to the picnic table to start filling a plate for him.

I'm halfway through scooping Leila's potato salad onto the plate when Oakleigh storms up to me. "Why are you hitting on Duke in front of the whole fire crew?" she snaps.

I spin around fast. "What?! I wasn't hitting on him."

"I saw you!" Her voice starts to rise. "I saw you holding his hand in the parking lot and now you're batting your eyelashes in his face. You better not be trying to get together with him!"

"What are you talking about?!" I counter. "I never held his hand anywhere—and I was just talking to him the same way I talk to everyone else."

"I just saw you!" Her voice rises to a shriek. "How can you spit on my dad's grave like this?! I thought I could trust you. He's barely dead and you're out there throwing yourself at someone else!"

I start to say, "Oakleigh...." but there's no reasoning with her.

"If you have to get with someone, why can't you get with Vince?" she blurts out. "He obviously likes you. At least he isn't a total stranger we don't even know."

"Duke is not a stranger—and I wasn't hitting on him. I was trying to welcome him to the barbecue when his wife is in a coma." I pull myself together with an effort. "I'm not going to talk to you about this. What I do is my business, not yours. Now, if you aren't going to get yourself something to eat....."

"I hate you!" she shrieks. "You're betraying my dad! You never loved him—and you never loved me! You're just playing an act before you can dump me on someone else and move on! I never should have trusted you! Get out of my life! You're a traitorous snake! I wish my dad never met you!"

I open my mouth to say something else, but she's glaring at me and raving so badly that I think better of it. I wouldn't be able to talk any sense into her about this.

She rushes toward me, narrows her eyes, and opens her mouth to launch into another full-scale assault. Her hair flies around her head and whips in her face like she might really be about to attack me.

I dread whatever she says next. Everyone stands around listening to her outburst.

Right then, Keith appears out of nowhere, wraps his beefy arms around Oakleigh, lifts her off the ground, and barges away across the beach taking her with him.

He growls once, "That's enough out of you, sweetheart. You're coming with me," and heads off for the parking lot.

She explodes into full, hysterical bellows, shrieks, and struggling to get out of his arms. She kicks, punches, and thrashes, but she can't get away.

Everyone stares in silence while he hauls her kicking and screaming to the parking lot, stuffs her into the cab of his truck, and drives off with her.

Her voice gets farther and farther away. It leaves a deadly silence behind it. No one moves or even breathes for a second.

"I shouldn't have come," Duke murmurs into that silence. "This was a mistake. I'm sorry."

He turns away. No one stops him from walking off to the parking lot and leaving, too.

I should go after him. I should apologize for Oakleigh's behavior and insist that none of this is his fault.

I can't move. I can't even think about what I should do about Oakleigh.

I'm supposed to be her legal guardian. I'm her stepmother and I'm responsible both for her welfare and her behavior.

I can't even decide what to do about her. It's my responsibility to straighten her out and make her behave, but I can't.

Maybe that's the problem. I'm too close to her and her grief. I understand and sympathize with her too much. I want to take it easy on her because I know how much she's hurting.

I can't do any of that. I can't do anything.

Minutes or even hours might have passed. I can't tell. Eventually, Brooke, Jessie, and Chris come over to me and pretend to accidentally bump into me when they get their food from the picnic table.

Their presence brings me back to reality, but it doesn't solve any of my problems. Nothing can—nothing except actually solving them.

I don't even want to think about whatever is going on between Keith and Oakleigh. I don't want to face her, but I know I have to. Just don't ask me what will happen then.

Chapter 6: Ellen

I take a deep breath and try to steady my nerves, but I still feel myself shaking. I have to sit in my car and think about how I'm going to face this before I bring myself to get out.

I stare at Keith's house through the windshield. Oakleigh is in there. The barbecue is long over. Now it's time for all of us to face the music.

I puff out my cheeks, open my door, and get out of the car. I march up to the front door a lot more bravely than I feel.

I knock and Leila answers. She isn't holding Leon for a change.

She smiles at me and then hugs me. "Hi. Come on in. Thanks for coming over."

"Thanks," I mumble and then, once I get across the threshold, I have to face Keith.

He sits on the couch while Leon lies on his stomach on the floor. He swims his little arms and legs around, bobs his head, and makes gurgling noises.

Keith keeps bending down every now and then to rub Leon's back to let the baby know that Keith is there.

Then Keith looks up at me. His eyes say it all.

He stands up just long enough to hug me. "How are you doing?"

"I'm scared out of my wits if you really want to know the truth," I murmur. "How did I get so scared of an eleven-year-old girl?"

"She got pretty nasty at the barbecue. My dad would have given her the hiding of her life for talking to an adult like that."

I look up at him. "Really? John never said anything about that."

"He apparently didn't say anything to Oakleigh about it, either. Maybe he didn't want her to be exposed to anything like that—or maybe she never acted up enough for him to mention it." He makes a face toward the side hall leading to the bedrooms. "I told her when I brought her home. I told her she's damn lucky to have you and she better start appreciating that she even has you at all."

I sink onto the couch shaking with nervous tension. "I really appreciate you stepping in the way you did. I really don't know what to do about her."

"Maybe it really is time for her to move in with someone else," Leila suggests. "She's missing her dad's influence. Maybe she needs a strong male role model in her life to take his place."

"I thought of that, but she's so insistent on staying with me—and it isn't like she doesn't already have Keith and Danny in her life. I mean, today proved that, didn't it?"

"What do you want to do?" Keith asks me. "I mean, what do *you* want to do? Just forget for a minute about what she wants. What would be the best thing for *you*? I don't want you to keep taking care of her if this is all too much for you."

"I don't want you to take care of her, either," I counter. "You and Leila already have your own family to worry about."

"We aren't talking like that," Keith snaps. "We're family and you're a part of that. If she needs to come here, then we'll just deal with it. We can't let you go down along with her. If moving her somewhere else is what's best for you, then that's what we have to do. It seems like she's already wearing you down and causing you way more stress than you need." He shoots the bedrooms another dirty look. "I already told her that, too, by the way. She really needs to pull it together."

I find myself laughing from nerves. "Thank you. I really appreciate your intervention."

"She can't just pity herself and make everyone else around her suffer," he goes on. "She can't express her grief by making your life miserable. That isn't on the list of acceptable options. She needs to learn to value you and to treat you accordingly. She wants to stay with you, but I think we should all make it clear that staying with you is a privilege that comes with certain conditions. She has to treat you right or we'll take her away from you. I don't see any other way to deal with her behavior."

I cringe at those words. "All right. If you think that's the best way to deal with it, then I'll go along with it."

"You agree with me, don't you?" he counters. "You must. You can't keep letting her treat you like this. It's unacceptable. John dying is not an excuse for her to wipe her ass with the people who care about her the most."

"Keith!" Leila murmurs.

"Well, it's true! I would never let a kid of mine treat another adult like this—and she basically is my kid. I'm her legal guardian, aren't I? She's my responsibility as much as anyone's—and she's my dead brother's daughter! I can't let her go down in flames like this. That wouldn't be right."

"Leila is right," I breathe. "Oakleigh really needs a strong male role model like you. You should make the decision on this. I don't seem to be able to think clearly when it comes to her. I can't make any decision and this sounds like the best alternative."

He narrows his eyes at me, compresses his lips, and nods once. "All right. We'll do it. We have to do something."

He stands up, steps over Leon, and goes down the hall to the first bedroom. He opens the door without knocking.

"Ellen is here to pick you up, Oakleigh," he says into the room. "Come on out."

Keith stands by the bedroom door until Oakleigh comes out. She takes one look at me and looks away.

That one moment gives me all the time I need to see the look of pure terror in her eyes. She's absolutely petrified.

"Take a seat, sweetheart," Keith tells her in his deep, rumbling voice. "We need to talk about a few things before you go home."

Oakleigh inches into the room looking at everything and everyone in rapid, terrified glances.

Leon makes a few squawking noises, so Keith picks up the baby, sits back down on the couch, and puts Leon on his shoulder. Then Keith lays Leon on his back on the couch next to him.

Keith rests his big hand on the baby's chest and stomach while Leon stares up at him from below.

Oakleigh sits in another armchair adjacent to the couch. She perches on the edge of the seat and squashes her hands between her knees.

I feel like I'm being sent to the principal's office—like Keith is about to tell me off as much as her.

He's right. I do need someone to tell me off. Oakleigh needs a parent right now, not a friend.

"Ellen and I were just talking about you living with her....." Keith begins.

Oakleigh spins around fast. "I have to live with her! You can't take me away from her! I told you I want to live with her! I don't want to live with you or Danny! I told you that!"

"We aren't talking about what you want," he counters. "We're talking about what's best for you. It's up to us as the adults in your life to decide what's best for you. If we decide that living with Ellen isn't what's best for you, then you won't live with her. Get that through your head right now. You're a child. We're the adults. We make the decisions—not you."

She cringes at his tone and cowers deeper into her chair. I really don't blame her. His tone makes me cringe, too.

"Now listen to me very carefully," he rumbles even lower. "I'm going to tell you the decision that we made and you're going to follow it. Is that understood?"

She looks away. "Yeah, okay."

"You can continue to live with Ellen, but only on certain conditions. You're going to stop all this rudeness, disrespect, and bad attitude. You're going to do everything she tells you to do without rolling your eyes, gasping, or making nasty remarks about it. You aren't going to yell at her or argue with her or insult her or anything like that. If I hear from her that you're doing any of that, we'll move you somewhere else. Got that? This isn't up for debate. You're on probation with no more strikes left. One more strike and you're out."

She looks down at her hands. "I know I messed up at the barbecue....."

"You did a lot more than mess up," he counters. "You're lucky we're sending you back to her at all after the way you've been acting. We shouldn't give you another chance. You've been treating Ellen like dog shit ever since your dad died."

"But...." She looks up with tears in her eyes and then they streak down her cheeks. Her lips start to tremble. She glances at me only once and immediately looks away. "But....what if she gets with someone else.....and I'm all alone....."

She breaks down sobbing right there on the chair. I can't stand to see her in pain.

I shift over to the arm of the chair, but I can't sit there very well with my brace in the way. I wind up sitting on the coffee table.

I hug her and kiss her hair. "I would never let that happen, sweetheart. You'll never lose me. You'll stay with me as long as you want to stay with me. I swear it. I would never leave you alone."

She finally breaks down enough to put her arms around me and wails into my shirt. "I can't stand the idea of you getting with someone else! You're all I have left!"

"I'm right here with you, sweetie!" I tell her. "I'm not going anywhere for a long time. I promise."

Keith doesn't interject to remind her that she wouldn't be alone because she would have him, Danny, and their families.

Keith doesn't say a word while I hold her until she calms down.

He deals with the baby and then hands Leon off to Leila, who takes the baby out of the room. Keith leans back on the couch and waits for Oakleigh to pull herself together.

She straightens up and I move back to my chair, but I sit on the edge of it, too. I want to stay as near her as I can. I don't want to leave her even to sit across the room from her.

I ache for this girl—probably because she's the one person who is still trapped in grief over John. Maybe some part of me wants to stay trapped there with her.

She wipes the tears off her cheeks and looks down at her hands knitting together in her lap. "Why did it have to be Duke?" she mumbles. "Why couldn't you just go out with Vince instead? He's nice. At least he isn't a stranger."

"Duke is not a stranger," Keith interjects. "He's part of the firehouse family just like everyone else—and he needs our support right now. You might at least think of someone who is going through the worst time of his life right now. You might have the decency not to make it worse for him than it already is."

I lean forward to squeeze her hands in her lap. "I'm not ready to get together with anyone, sweetheart. I already told Vince that. I'm not interested in anyone. I'm just trying to keep the lights on, take care of you, and stay sane. Getting over your dad is hard enough right now."

She looks up at me with swimming eyes. "Really?"

"Of course. You didn't think I just forgot about him, did you? I have to keep going so I take care of you and the house and everything. That's the only reason I'm doing any of this. I would be a puddle of tears on the floor if I didn't."

"But.....you always act like everything is fine. You don't cry about it. You even laugh and have fun."

I have to smile at her, but it's a sad smile. I even find my eyes stinging. "I have to act that way, sweetie. It's the only way I can keep going without him. I wish I could fall apart. I really wish I could. Every day is a nightmare without him, but I wouldn't be much good to you if I didn't keep things running."

I brush away a tear. I can't fall back into that.

She stares at me in wide-eyed wonder. "I thought you were trying to forget him. I thought you were trying to move on."

"I am—but only because I have to. I try to forget him because I can't forget him. I'll never be able to forget him. He was....." I break off and choke on tears.

Keith saves the situation by interrupting again. "You two can talk about this at home. You remember what I said, sweetheart. You living with Ellen comes with rules and standards of behavior. You break the rules—you don't get to live with Ellen. You treat her with respect. You help her out. You give her a good, helpful attitude. The way you've been acting makes me think you shouldn't live with her at all. If you want to keep living with her, you're going to have to convince all of us otherwise. Understand?"

She nods down at the floor.

"Then you two better go home," he tells us. "It's a school night. Get some sleep. We can talk about this later."

Chapter 7: Duke

I stand across the room from Naomi's hospital bed and stare down at her still body. What the hell am I even doing here?

She never moves. She never opens her eyes. She never squeezes my hand when I touch her.

I've only tried touching her hand three times since the accident. Her hand feels dead and creepy to me.

I can't stand touching her like this. I can't stand seeing her like this. Everything about this makes my skin crawl.

I shouldn't be here. I should be at the firehouse. At least I can do something with my life and make a difference there.

I don't know for sure, but my presence there seems to help the crew, too. They would keep working without me. I know that.

The atmosphere around the firehouse isn't so much of a cemetery when I'm there. They all know what I'm going through, but we all pretend I'm not.

I can't believe how supportive everyone is being. I don't know why I'm surprised because we've all gone through it with them. Now it's my turn.

It kills me to know the effort they're all making to help me maintain the illusion. They're all hurting over Naomi, too, but the crew goes about their business and even jokes around as if none of this is happening.

I love them for that. I should go back there. Coming here only messes with my head.

Nothing will ever go back to the way things were between me and Naomi. We lost Amelia. We lost the baby.

Naomi doesn't even have a uterus anymore. She'll be absolutely devastated if she ever wakes up and finds out.

I don't look forward to that, but I look forward to our married life after that even less. I could have children with someone else, but I don't want to. I want her and now I'll never get her back—not the way it was before.

The dream is dead. We had such a beautiful dream of raising a family together.

We lived that dream together for eight blissful months. Now that's gone, too, just like Amelia.

Someone appears at my side and rests their small hand on my back. It's Ellen. I can't even look at her.

She doesn't say a word. She doesn't stoop so low as to ask if I'm okay.

She needs support as much as I do and yet she's here with me. I wish I could say something to thank her for everything she's doing, but I can't bring myself to say anything.

She stands next to me in silence staring down at Naomi just like I am. There's nothing to do. Naomi's condition never changes.

She'll probably never come out of this coma. The doctors are already talking about taking her off the ventilator. I'm starting to wish they would just hurry up and do it.

Naomi is already dead. Having this corpse lying in a hospital bed is just making it harder for me to move on. It's making it impossible for me to move on.

I can't grieve for her or Amelia or our baby as long as Naomi is still here. Whatever this half-life is that she's living—it holds me in suspension. I can't think or move or plan anything or even hardly breathe as long as she's still here.

Ellen finally squeezes my shoulder. "Let's get out of here," she murmurs. "I'll take you down to the cafeteria and we can get a cup of coffee or something. Come on. Don't hang around here."

I don't want to hang around here, but I still find it hard to leave.

As soon as I walk into Naomi's hospital room, I switch into this frozen state where nothing else exists. I need another person to pull me out of it.

Ellen leaves her hand on my arm to anchor me to reality. How does she always know exactly what I need?

She's my lifeline in all of this. She's my oxygen hose that will lead me back to the boat when I'm floating adrift in the ocean of mindless devastation.

She would probably take my hand if I really needed her to.

I turn away. I wouldn't be able to break away from staring at Naomi if Ellen wasn't here.

I just have to follow her out of this room. Then I'll be fine.

I don't want to go to the cafeteria. I don't want to sit across the table from Ellen Foreman and have her look into my eyes. That would be the worst.

I don't want her to see how hard this is for me, but I know I need that, too. I need someone to see it and she's the only one I can let see it.

We get as far as the door before the ICU team comes in from outside. They surround Naomi to adjust all her IV levels, take her vitals, move and exercise her limbs, check her ET tube, give her a sponge bath, and perform all other details of her care that she needs.

Ellen and I have to move out of the way to let the team enter the room. We have to flatten ourselves against the wall so the team can get their carts of supplies inside.

They swarm Naomi's bed and leave the doorway clear. Now Ellen and I can go. I don't want to stick around for this part.

Ellen turns away, too, but right at that moment, the ECG machine next to Naomi's bed lets out a loud beep—and the beep doesn't stop.

Ellen and I turn around. It takes one split second for both of us to see that Naomi's heart rate isn't a steady sinus rhythm anymore.

The team goes into a frenzy. I hear them yelling the words from a great distance away. *She's coding.*

I rush in to get to her. I have to do something. I have to fix it. I have to treat her. I have to give her the drugs to save her life.

Ellen grabs me and holds me back. I try to fight her off, but she turns out to be really strong even though she's so much smaller than I am.

She pushes me hard enough to slam me against the wall. That blow knocks enough sense into my brain for the volume to switch back on.

The ICU team revolves around Naomi's bed shooting her full of a million drugs, but nothing works.

Someone starts doing compressions and they hook her up to a defibrillator, but the first shock only sends her deeper into cardiac arrest.

I stand frozen in shock watching this. Ellen leans all her weight against me to hold me against the wall so I don't rush in and interfere.

I wouldn't be able to do anything anyway. The team is already doing everything.

I hear every order for every drug and every intervention they're doing to her. There is nothing more to do......and then the line of her heart rate goes flat. It doesn't come back.

The team backs off. The nurses, residents, technicians, and medics say a few more things to each other and then leave the room.

Ellen and I stay where we are on the side of the room watching it all. Even she seems frozen in time.

I feel her leaning on me even when she doesn't have to. We both stare at Naomi lying motionless on the bed.

She looks exactly the same as before. The ET tube sticks out of her mouth. The electrodes run from her chest to the ECG machine. The IV still goes into her arm.

She looks just as dead as she did before except that the ventilator no longer pumps air into her lungs to make her breathe.

I want to leave. Now I have no reason to stay here. I push myself off the wall and turn back to the door in a numb trance.

I don't need to be here for the part where the hospital staff takes all that crap off her and leaves her lying on the bed like she's asleep or something.

I don't need to be here anymore at all ever again. Good. I never have to come back here. I can bury myself in work and forget all of this ever happened.

I can forget that I ever met Naomi....and that we adopted Amelia....and that they gave me hope that I could have a family the way I always wanted.

Just thinking about them makes tears spring to my eyes, and before I can even think to stop it, a bottomless well of rage and betrayal explodes out of me beyond anything I ever thought possible.

I never let myself feel this before. I never let myself understand how truly furious I was about all of this.

Amelia got blown up when that car exploded. My unborn baby got crushed against the steering column when the airbag failed. Naomi suffered fatal injuries when that truck squashed her body against the dashboard.

How could any of that happen? Naomi was a sweet, kind, caring woman who only wanted to dedicate herself to me and her children.

She never hurt anyone. She spent her life saving people before she became a mother.

Amelia and the baby never hurt anyone. None of them deserved any of this—and I don't deserve any of this.

I spin away from Ellen to stop her from seeing, but it's too late. I hurl myself against the wall roaring out all my pain and rage, but nothing will ever make it go away.

I smash my fist into the wall again and again, but I'm crying too hard even to feel the pain or notice if I'm damaging hospital property.

I want to hurt someone for doing this to the people I most love, but I want to hurt myself more. I want to feel any pain other than what I'm actually feeling.

Naomi really is gone. It's all gone. Everything I cared about—all the hopes I pinned on them—all gone.

Ellen comes up behind me, but I'm raging too much to let her touch me. I whip around and actually lash out at her before I think to stop myself.

I try to pull back, but I can't control anything. I cover my face to try to pull myself back from the brink, but that only seems to make me cry harder.

As soon as I cover my eyes, all my rage dies. This is somehow so much worse than crying over Amelia.

I can finally cry for all three of them now. They're all gone. I'm completely alone.

Thinking that brings such a depth of anguish that I can't stand it. I howl with sobs. I can't think or even see.

I stagger farther back into the room and bump into something. I hear crashing, but I really don't care.

This agony will never stop. I've never been this alone in my life. The people I would turn to for help and comfort are all gone.

No one will be waiting for me at home ever again. I won't hurry home from work to see my baby girl.

God, I used to love going home knowing that Naomi and Amelia were waiting for me there!

I don't know half the things I'm thinking and feeling right now. I'm so mad I can't feel how much this hurts, but I'm hurting too much even to feel mad.

Out of nowhere, Ellen takes hold of my shoulders and pulls me forward. She doesn't even try to reason with me, thank the stars.

She pulls me out of that awful room. Thank God Almighty someone is here to deal with this. Of course she knows exactly what I need.

She steers me down the corridor toward the exit doors leaving ICU. I don't need to be here anymore, but I can't even think clearly enough to decide to leave. I can't think anything except that I'm completely alone in the world.

I have nothing. I'm no one. My life is over. I might as well be dead, too. I died on that bed.

I take my hands down when we get out of ICU, but I'm still crying too hard to stop. Maybe I'll never stop. I don't see how I can. I don't see how I can even survive this.

Ellen doesn't let go of me. She pulls me out of the building and out to the parking lot. She takes out her keys on the way there, presses the button on her key fob to unlock the doors, and opens the door to her car before she pushes me into the passenger seat.

I collapse sobbing on the seat. I'm too wrecked even to put on my seat belt, but she doesn't interrupt me to tell me to do it.

I can only stare into space and look at the vast wreckage that is my life. It's over. There's nothing left of me or anything else.

I'll keep working as Fire Chief as soon as I stop crying.

That's all I have left—the job. I don't even exist anymore.

She drives me across town. I really wish I could keep crying forever, but of course it doesn't work out that way.

She pulls into the driveway of her house—John Brewer's old house. She lives here with Oakleigh now.

She gets out, opens the passenger door, and pulls me out by the elbow. My brain doesn't function well enough even to resist that.

She steers me around like a child. That's what I am. I'm not a person anymore. I need a competent, responsible adult to deal with all of this. God knows I can't.

She takes me inside and sits me down on the couch before she sits down next to me. She doesn't say anything for a long time.

I stare down at my hands. Who even am I anymore? What is my life even worth? I wouldn't go on if I didn't have the job. The firehouse needs a Chief.

Keith could do the job, but it's my job. I wouldn't want to let the crew down by opting out.

Ellen reads my mind, goes into the other room, and I hear her talking on the phone.

"Hi, sweetheart. It's me. I just came from the hospital. Duke was there visiting Naomi and she coded right in front of him. Could you tell the crew that she's gone? Yeah, Duke is a disaster. I brought him to my house until he calms down. Could you cover the firehouse?

Thanks. I'm sure he appreciates knowing he can count on you. Yeah, I'll tell him you said so. No, I can't get a word out of him right now. It could be a while. He isn't doing too good. Great. Thanks, sweetie. Bye."

She comes back into the living room and sits down next to me again.

She waits in silence for a long time before she breaks it. She's right. I do appreciate that I can rely on Keith to take over for me. Who else would she call?

"I think you should stay here for a while," she tells me in a low murmur. "You don't have to go back to your place and you don't have to go to the firehouse until you're ready. You can stay as long as you want to."

I don't answer. I wish I could, but I don't even have a voice anymore. I'm just a shell.

This must be what Ellis went through after John Brewer got shot. There is no me left to speak to any of these people. There's just the job. That has to be enough.

She goes into the kitchen and leaves me sitting there alone.

I stare down at my hands and watch silent tears falling onto them. Naomi. Amelia. The baby. All gone. Everything is gone.

I can't even bring myself to wish that I never gotten involved with Naomi. I could never wish that Amelia hadn't come into my life.

I could never wish that the last nine months never happened. Just thinking about them makes me want to cry—not because they're gone, but because they happened in the first place.

God, they made me so happy! I loved them so much. I loved them with my whole being. I never knew I could love anyone that much.

Just sitting here loving them makes me cry. I love them more than anything. My heart breaks with how much I love them still.

Their love changed me. It changed everything for me. I'm somehow more of a man because of that love.

It almost feels like I can die now because I experienced that love at least once in my life. It didn't even have to come to anything. It happened and now it lies here branded into my flesh.

I didn't have to see Amelia grow up. I didn't have to walk her down the aisle on her wedding day.

I didn't have to watch Naomi give birth to our baby and go through the stress of helping her raise another baby and maybe a few more.

It happened.

I remember the words Naomi and I said when Amelia first came home to us. We agreed we would love her and give her our absolute best for as long as it lasted.

We agreed we would never let a day or a night go by when she didn't know she was loved. She would always know she had two parents who would do absolutely anything for her—and we did it.

She experienced that love for the first nine months of her life—the only nine months of her life.

We surrounded her in that love from the day she was born until the day she died. She never lived one hour on this planet without that love and constant support.

Naomi and the baby had it, too. We did what we could for as long as it lasted.

That baby came into existence in love. It came into existence with two parents who loved it more than life itself. That baby spent its short time on Earth surrounded in all the love we could possibly give.

Just thinking those words makes me dissolve in silent tears all over again. For as long as it lasts.

I can let all three of them go because I loved them for as long as they were mine to love. I gave them my all. I can be proud that I did my best for them in the time we had together.

I can't ask more of myself than that and I don't. I was a good husband to Naomi and a good father to Amelia and the baby.

I'm a good father because I'm sitting here crying over them. I have nothing to be ashamed of in anything I did or anything I do.

I only have to think about Keith Brewer. He's such a good father. He would approve of everything I did and everything I do.

He would sit here and comfort me if he was here. It just happens to be Ellen.

It somehow means more coming from him because he's such a good father. He gets it.

He has been my main source of support through all of this. I cry even out of gratitude that I had his help and friendship when I needed it.

He'll support me even more now because I'm living his worst nightmare. Nothing could be worse than this. No one knows it better than he does.

Chapter 8: Ellen

I pull up my car in front of the school and Oakleigh dives into the front seat. She throws her backpack on the floor and pulls on her seatbelt as I steer away into the traffic of all the other parents picking up their kids.

"Hey, munchkin," I greet her. "How did that day go?"

"My teacher wants to have a meeting with you," she tells me.

"What is the meeting about?" I glance at her out of the corner of my eye. She better not be getting into trouble at school.

That would be the worst—if she started acting out at school.

She's been withdrawn and isolated up until now. I almost hope she stays that way.

"She wants to talk to you about a paper I wrote about Dad. We got a writing assignment to write about a dream we have. That was the whole assignment. I wrote about the nightmare I keep having of Andy shooting Dad at the beach." She rolls her eyes at me. "That was the assignment. She didn't say it had to be a dream about our future plans or anything like that. She got all snotty by saying I deliberately twisted the assignment around to make it something bad—and then she actually had the nerve to suggest that I made the whole thing up to get attention." She crosses her arms over her chest, throws herself back in the seat, and glares out the window at the other kids. "Now she wants to talk to you about my behavior."

"Have you gotten into trouble in any other way or is this the first time?"

"I never did anything!" she blurts out. "I don't even want to talk to people. Now she's making a huge thing about how I don't volunteer to answer in class the way I used to. She thinks there's something wrong with me because I don't want to talk to anyone or participate in class. Why can't she just leave me alone? I did the assignment. I did exactly what she said. I have that dream every night. What the hell does she want?"

"Okay, can we not start using swear words about it? I'll talk to her—and I think you did the right thing by writing the assignment about that."

She spins around to stare at me. "You do?! Really?"

"Of course. You should write it out. You should write about what happened and all your feelings about it. It will be a good way for you to process all the memories and all your unresolved feelings. I almost wish I had thought of it sooner."

She blinks at me. "Really?!"

"Of course. You should start a journal about it. Then you won't have to worry about other people being horrified that you have these pictures in your head."

She looks away again. "I didn't know I could do that."

I extend my hand across the seat and squeeze her arm. "There is nothing wrong with you writing about it. It's a good way for you to express your thoughts and talk about what happened. I know you have a hard time doing that with people. Writing is the perfect solution."

She doesn't answer nor does she look at me.

I don't say anything all the way back to the house.

I hate to think what images she has floating around in her head from John's death. It was traumatic enough for me, the Brewer brothers, and everyone from the fire crew to see John get shot like that.

Oakleigh is just a child. She never should have seen anyone lying dead on the ground like that with their head blasted off, much less her own father.

I pull into the driveway. She starts picking up her backpack.

I stop her by laying my hand on her arm again. "Hold it, sweetie. I need to talk to you. Duke is inside."

She whips around again and narrows her eyes at me. "Why?"

"Because Naomi died today and he's really upset. I happened to be there at the hospital when it happened. He was a mess, so I brought him here. He needed somewhere to go where he could deal with it. This seemed like the best place."

"You didn't have to bring him here!" she snaps. "Why couldn't you take him to his house?"

I make a face. "He shared that house with Naomi and Amelia. The house would have reminded him of her. I couldn't take him there."

"You didn't have to bring him here!" she rages. "This is my house! I don't want him here."

My mind switches gears. Keith might finally have talked some sense into my head.

I lower my voice to a dangerous undertone. "Duke is a part of the firehouse family, Oakleigh. He just lost his wife, his baby daughter, and his unborn child. He'll stay here as long as he needs to and you will do everything in your earthly power to help him. If staying here helps him at all, then you'll do it. Is that clear? If you can't at least be nice to him, then go to your room, shut the door, and stay there. He doesn't need that kind of headache from you or anyone else right now. You might be a little more sympathetic after what you're going through with your dad. You might show a little compassion to someone who is going through the same thing."

She narrows her eyes at me in a cruel scowl. "You better not get together with him."

"Who I get together with is none of your business, young lady. I'm an adult. You don't tell me what I can and can't do. Keith told you that you're on probation. Don't make this the straw that ends things between us."

She whirls away from me, throws open the door, yells, "I hate you!" and takes off running down the block. She doesn't even shut the door behind her.

I slump in my seat and cover my eyes. Great. As if Duke doesn't have a hard enough time already.

I'll be damned if I let Oakleigh make it worse for him. Keith is so right about this. She's a child. She needs to get it together. Her own pain is no excuse to hurt others, especially not a man in Duke's situation.

I wait a few minutes before I get out of the car, shut the passenger door, get back behind the wheel, and reverse out of the driveway.

It doesn't take me long to find Oakleigh. She walks her fastest, but her legs aren't long enough to take her very far.

I spot her down the street on her way past the school. A bunch of kids play on the playground, but of course she doesn't go there.

I inch down the street at a distance so she won't see me. She doesn't even turn around.

She eventually turns in at Danny's house. Good. He'll deal with this.

I follow until I glide my car up to the curb. I'm just turning off the motor when my phone rings. It's him. Of course.

I answer it. "Is this the city animal control officer?"

He laughs on the other end of the line. "I have a rabid wildcat in my house."

"I'm really sorry about this. I'm parked outside. I'll come in and get her."

"Don't," he tells me. "Leave her here. She needs to cool down. Maybe being here will show her what it would be like if she actually came to live here. Maybe she needs that kind of perspective right now."

I heave an almighty sigh. "I hope you're right."

"What happened?" he asks. "What was it this time?"

"Naomi coded today. She's gone. She died right in front of Duke and he was an absolute wreck. I just happened to be there at the time. I had to get him out of the hospital, so I took him to our house. I just picked up Oakleigh from school and took her home. I stopped her in the driveway to tell her that Duke was there and she got nasty. I tried to get stern with her and tell her to at least show some compassion to someone who is going through the same thing she went through with her dad. She's fixated on this idea that Duke and I are together and we're going to cut her out. It's nuts."

"Which part is nuts—the idea of you and Duke getting together or her being worried that you're going to cut her out?"

"All of it! I mean, I would never get together with Duke...."

"Why not?" Danny asks. "You could do a lot worse. The guy is a damn king."

I gasp out loud. "Danny! Stop it!"

"What?" he asks. "You have great taste in men. You only like the best. Who better than him?"

"His wife just died a few hours ago and you're already trying to set me up with him?! What the hell?! Besides, I'm not ready to move on from John. There's nothing going on between me and Duke and there never will be."

"Maybe there should be," he tells me. "Maybe Oakleigh is onto something here—or maybe she sees something you don't."

"She doesn't see anything because there's nothing to see! I've just been trying to help him and support him. Somebody has to and I just happened to be there both of the times he needed someone—and before you start talking about cosmic synchronicity or something, I was only there because I work at the hospital. I'm sure exactly the same thing would have happened if Keith or anyone from the firehouse had been there."

"Maybe, but I still think it makes sense. Either way, it isn't for Oakleigh to say anything against it."

I let out another shaky breath. "So you're okay with her staying there?"

"Of course. The longer the better in my opinion. She obviously isn't ready to deal with you and what all that means. Maybe you were right and you two shouldn't be together after all."

"I really don't want to think about that....like....ever."

His voice softens. "You know where we are if you need us. You should take some time off from being her stepmother and just concentrate on taking care of yourself. You need that as much as she does if not more. You've been there for her this whole time. You shut yourself down so you could take care of her. Take some time to just deal with your own stuff. Let me and Keith handle her for a change."

My throat constricts. I can't even speak to answer him. Of course he and Keith know how it is.

Danny doesn't even ask if I'm okay. He knows I'm not.

His voice softens even more if that's possible. "Go home, sweetheart," he murmurs. "Don't worry about her or us. Everything is under control. We're right here if you need anything."

He doesn't wait for me to answer before he hangs up. I wouldn't have been able to hang up if he didn't do it first.

As soon as I put the phone down, I break down crying right there in the seat. I cover my face and let the tears out.

He's so right. Why do all these people have to know me so well?

I never let myself feel the pain of John's death. I used Oakleigh to mask it.

Now I have to go home to an empty house and face my life without him. I've been using Oakleigh to run away from this. I wanted to keep her with me and keep taking care of her so I wouldn't have to be alone.

I cry all the way home and don't stop until I park in the driveway.

I have to pull it together before I go in there and deal with Duke. He doesn't need to see me emotional.

The thought of helping him does the trick for me to put my own feelings aside. Maybe I'm just a perpetual caregiver.

I check my eyes in the visor mirror. They don't look too bloodshot. I blow my nose and go in.

Duke isn't in the living room. I just left him there when I went to pick up Oakleigh.

I check the whole house, but he isn't here. He must have left while I was out. Now he's gone.

Chapter 9: Duke

I push open a box, use my packing tape dispenser to secure the bottom, and put the box on the floor.

I start taking toys and other stuff off the shelf and throwing everything in the box. This is Amelia's room even though she never slept in here.

This is where Naomi and I kept all Amelia's clothes, diapers, toys, blankets, and all the other baby stuff. We planned to make this Amelia's room when she got old enough to sleep in a bed by herself.

I fill that box and start on a second one. As soon as I finish packing up all the baby gear, I go to the living room, open another box, and start clearing all the stuff off the shelves in there, too.

I'm in the middle of that when I hear someone knock on the front door. I didn't hear anyone pull up.

I find out why when I open it. Ellen stands outside. She didn't pull into the driveway. She parked at the curb like a stranger.

She gives me a strange look. "Are you okay? I mean, don't answer that. I was worried when I came home and didn't find you at my place."

She glances behind me. Her expression changes when she sees all the boxes.

"I'm fine," I clip in what I hope won't be too harsh a tone. "I'm just packing up all the baby gear and some of this other stuff."

I can't stand the way she's looking at me, so I turn away and go back over to the shelf.

She takes a step into the room to follow me. She only has to glance around once to see all the baby gear in boxes. Now I'm starting on everything else in this house.

Half of it is Naomi's stuff. I put pictures of her family in a separate box. Her family will probably want all of that back.

The rest of it I'll get rid of. I'll either donate it to the thrift stores or dump it.

The sound of the tape dispenser startles me into spinning around. I stare as Ellen tapes up another box, sets it on the dining room table, and starts putting all my books into it.

"What are you doing?" I ask.

"You're packing up. I'm helping you." She reads the spines of some of the books. "I don't blame you for wanting to get the hell out of here and go scorched Earth on everything. I really wanted to after John died, but I had to leave everything the way it was for Oakleigh's sake. I never wanted to see that shit again. Leaving everything the way it was somehow made everything a thousand times harder."

She goes right back to loading the books into the box. I can't watch, so I go back to my own job. "Thanks," I mumble. "I just want to sell this house and never set foot in it again."

"I don't blame you. Where will you stay?"

"I don't know," I mutter. "I really don't care as long as it isn't here. I guess I'll stay in a motel room until I can rent something. I'll buy another house after this one sells. I don't care as long as it isn't this."

"You're welcome to stay with us if you want to. You don't need to stay in a motel. That might make it worse if it makes you think you're alone. At least, with us, you would have some people around who care about you." She shoots me a grin. "The food is better, too."

I can't look at her. "I'm sure Oakleigh would have something to say about me staying there."

She turns bright red and concentrates on taping up another box for all the books. "I really don't care if she does have something to say about it. You're family and you need us right now. She can deal with it. Besides, she's staying with Danny and Emily for a little while until she screws her head on straight about all of this."

I look up at her. "Are *you* okay?"

"Not really," she breezes. "I mean, not at all if you want to know the truth. I had a breakdown just before because Oakleigh wasn't there and I was going to have to go home to an empty house. I really have been using her as a shield to hide from my feelings about John. How pathetic is that—hiding behind a child so I don't have to face reality?"

"It isn't pathetic," I murmur. "It's totally normal."

She makes a face, but I definitely get the sense that she's avoiding eye contact with me.

Why did I think she didn't feel the pain the way I do? She kept functioning so she could take care of her stepdaughter—the same way I kept functioning so I could take care of the firehouse. We both hide behind something else.

She notices me staring at her extra hard. One minute, I can't look at her at all. Now I can't look away.

She raises her eyes to meet mine. "What?"

"Nothing," I murmur. "I really appreciate all of this—everything you're doing. You're the only person who really understands enough to talk to me about all of this."

She grimaces. Now I definitely see the hidden pain underneath it all. "I just wish I could do something to make it better for you even though I know I can't." She takes another handful of books off the shelf. "If this is all I can do, then that will have to be enough."

She lifts the box off the table, carries it across the room, and stacks it next to the boxes of baby gear.

I stare at her the whole way there. She can see all of Amelia's clothes and blankets piled in those boxes. There is no way Ellen doesn't see what I'm doing.

She goes back to the bookshelf, tapes up a third box, and starts loading that, too. I can't stand here doing nothing while she works.

I start packing up my own things from the shelf. "Thanks," I mumble again.

"Do you want to get rid of everything?" she asks over her shoulder. "I suppose you have no reason to keep Naomi's things."

"I was thinking I would send everything back to her family." I wince. "I can't stand to look at this stuff." I hesitate and then stop. "Maybe I shouldn't be doing this."

"Why not? You were sure before I showed up, weren't you? I didn't come over here to change your mind."

"I don't know," I mumble. "Maybe I thought I had to strike a blow against the world for my freedom. I guess I must have been kidding myself that no one would understand. I thought everyone would want to keep this place as some kind of monument to Naomi."

She snorts. "I don't blame you for wanting to tear that down. That would be a massive insult to you if they did."

I can't look at her. It somehow hurts so much worse that she understands.

I finish with the shelf and go into the kitchen. I have to use a separate box for the things I want to keep for the time when I get my new rental apartment.

Ellen works across the room from me until she finishes the bookshelf. I'm still working on the kitchen when she comes over.

She studies me across the counter for a minute until she gets my attention.

She waits until I actually look up and make eye contact. When she does bring herself to speak, she barely murmurs above an undertone. "Do you want me to clear out Naomi's clothes and things from your bedroom?"

I can't look at her or make a sound. I turn my head away and nod. I couldn't face the bedroom without losing my shit completely.

She doesn't say a word of acknowledgment. She turns her back on me, tapes up three boxes, and leaves the room.

I can't think about her putting Naomi's clothes and personal articles in a box that will disappear out of my life.

Of course Ellen must understand about all of that. Who helped her? Did she have to clean out John's clothes, shoes, belts, and toiletries by herself? I can't imagine anything worse than that.

My throat hurts from gratitude that she's doing this for me. Thank the stars in Heaven I have her.

I hear her opening and closing drawers in there. Then I hear her rummaging around in the bathroom. I try to pay attention to the kitchen so I don't think about what she's doing.

She comes back with the boxes completely taped shut so I can't see what's in them. She has scrawled on the outside, *Naomi's clothes,* or *Naomi's shoes,* or *Naomi's hair and bathroom gear.*

She stacks everything with the baby gear and books.

"Do you want me to pack up your stuff?" Ellen asks me. "I could at least get it out of the bedroom so you don't have to go in there. What do you think?"

"That would be great," I choke. "Thank you."

She doesn't say a word to that, either. She disappears into the bedroom and comes back with two big suitcases stuffed and zipped.

She parks them by the door. "You can take those to the motel. All your uniforms and casual clothes are in there."

I can't even speak to thank her.

She glances at her watch. She probably wants to leave now.

"Are you hungry?" she asks. "I could go get us some takeout. What do you think? I get it if you aren't hungry. I didn't eat for a week after John died."

"That would be great," I croak. "I am hungry. I just didn't trust myself to stop or I might not be able to start again."

She smiles at me and heads for the door. "Is Mexican okay with you?"

"Yeah," I husk. "Thanks."

She leaves and drives off. I can't believe this is happening. Life is so different with her helping me.

I get back to work and realize while I'm doing it that I actually feel better.

A massive weight lifts off my shoulders, now that I realize don't have to pack up the bedroom. I was really dreading that.

I go in there just to check. The place is completely stripped. She even took the sheets, blankets, and pillows off the bed.

The room looks like no one has ever lived here. She didn't leave a single thing in the bathroom, the closet, the dresser, in any of the drawers, or anywhere else. Everything is gone—exactly the way I wanted it to be.

I go back to the kitchen and then start taking things out of the garage. Most of the stuff in here is from my old house—the house I owned before I moved in with Naomi.

That house is long gone. I wouldn't want to go back there anyway.

I don't have to pack up the garage. I don't know if I'll keep this stuff, but it's already all packed up.

Ellen comes back. "Come out on the porch," she tells me. "We can eat out here."

I go sit next to her on the porch step while she unpacks the food she brought for both of us. She hands me an absolutely gargantuan burrito, a big box of loaded nachos, and lays out a container of churros between us.

Then she puts a big frosty cup of soda with a lid and a straw next to me and settles down to eat her burrito.

"Thank you for this," I mumble.

"Are you kidding me? I would have eaten takeout for the rest of my life if I didn't have Oakleigh. I kept setting the table for three and having to quickly scramble to take the place setting away before she saw." She shakes her head and makes a clucking noise. "Danny's right. I made this so much harder on myself than I needed to by taking care of her."

"Why would you say that?" I ask. "She needed you and you needed her. You still do. You both do. I'm sure she appreciates you for being there for her."

She makes a face. "I'm sure she would disagree with you about how much she appreciates it. She says she wants to live with me and doesn't want to live with anyone else, but her motives are probably as unhealthy as my motives for wanting to live with her." She looks away across the neighborhood. "Now she's staying at Danny's house and I have no choice but to face the music."

Her voice cracks with hidden pain. This is the first time I've ever seen her so vulnerable.

I don't know why I thought it would be any different for her. I wasn't around when she had to deal with the fallout from John's death. I didn't know these people then.

Why did I think it would be different for Keith and Danny? I know it wasn't. I just held the whole thing at a distance. I wasn't involved in any of it until long afterward.

I can't imagine what I would be doing if Ellen wasn't sitting here next to me right now. I probably wouldn't eat at all like she says.

She humanizes me. She brings me back from the edge of annihilation. I can actually appreciate the fact that I'm still alive even after this disaster.

She turns around to pick up her nachos. "When do you think you'll go back to work?"

"I don't know. Tomorrow, I suppose. The firehouse is really good for me. It's all I have to keep me going right now."

"I'm sure everyone would love to see you back. It would be good for you to be around the people who understand and care about you."

"I really wish John was still alive," I murmur. "I wish I could thank him for everything he's done for me. I can't imagine what my life would be like without the firehouse and everyone in it. I know he did all this. He's the one who got me Naomi. He got me all of this—and now he's the one getting me through it because all these people made me part of their family."

Her eyes well up with tears. "I'm really sorry for your loss. I know it doesn't mean anything to say so, but we're all here for you. We all feel for you....especially me."

She brushes tears off her cheeks and turns back all businesslike to her food.

She pretends that I can't see how much she's hurting, but it's okay because I understand. She doesn't have to cope in front of me any more than I have to cope in front of her.

This moment is such a priceless gift. I will never be able to repay any of this.

The good news is that I don't even have to try. She gives it freely out of her pure heart. They all do.

We eat in silence for what seems like a long time. I don't have to think of anything to say.

We finish eating. She packs up all the trash and adds it to the plastic garbage bag I've been using to throw away everything I don't plan to keep.

We both go back to work for another few hours. It's long past dark by the time we finish and I load my suitcases into the back of my truck.

"Thank you for all your help," I tell her again—like that means something at this point.

"Do you have a room lined up already or are you just going to get one now?"

"I'll just go get one now. I know a nice motel on the other side of town. I can stay there as long as I need to—and the rooms each have a small kitchenette. It will work until I can get a rental."

"Okay. Have a good night. Call me if you need anything." She takes a step toward me and raises her arms to hug me. "I mean it. Don't hesitate to call if anything happens."

"I won't." I hug her and find myself shutting my eyes in the deep gratitude I hold for her. "Thank you. You don't know how much this means to me."

She pulls away and makes a face again. "Don't worry about Oakleigh. Maybe Danny is right and her staying with someone else will give her the distance not to feel so petrified about me getting together with someone else."

"Is that what this is about? Is that why she accused you of hitting on me at the barbecue?"

"That's what she said. She's worried I'll find someone else and move on and leave her alone. If she stays with Danny, Zeke, and Emily for a while, maybe she'll realize she wouldn't be alone after all. Then maybe she'll stop dreading it."

I find myself studying her. I shouldn't considering that Naomi isn't even in the ground yet.

Ellen is so awesome. She's such a big-hearted, easy-going foundation stone of the whole firehouse culture.

She's everything great about this little community. I know now why John Brewer fell for her.

"How do *you* feel about moving on?" I ask. "Sorry. I shouldn't ask that. It's none of my business."

She actually turns bright red in front of me. "I'm not ready for that. I can't even get my own life in order. No one would want to share that."

I don't say anything. Her life looks pretty all right to me—not like mine.

She blushes again and her eyelashes dip when she sees me studying her. "I better go. I'll see you soon."

I watch her walk down the driveway to her car. She waves at me through the windshield before she drives off.

I stand outside in the driveway for a long time. Tonight changed me again. I can actually face this now.

I didn't think I would ever be able to, but she gave me that back. That is a debt I will never be able to repay if I live a thousand years.

I go back into the house alone before I leave. I stand around in the living room and take in the stripped shelves, the empty kitchen, and the piles of boxes.

All the bedrooms are empty. There's nothing left.

I never have to come back to this house thanks to Ellen's help. I'll move out all the boxes and then sell the house with all the furniture in it.

All the memories associated with this house will become someone else's problem.

This moment ends things for me. I can put this whole life behind me. I thought it would take longer for me to be okay with that, but I can do it now.

Ellen gave me a clean break. She made it happen in a day instead of the process dragging out for weeks.

I actually feel pretty good about things when I go outside, lock the front door, and get into my truck.

I take the house keys off my keychain and stick them in the unused ashtray in the dashboard before I drive off across town.

Chapter 10: Duke

I look up from my desk when the firehouse alarm goes off again. I've been trying to schedule interviews with the potential new hires, but as usual, that will have to wait.

I go out to the garage just as the trucks and ambulance pull out. I get into the support pickup and follow.

We pull up at a car accident scene, but it's pretty straightforward. One car sits on the sidewalk with its front end wrapped around a telephone pole.

There are two patients inside the driver's compartment. The crew doesn't have any problem extricating both of them.

I follow the ambulances to the hospital and pretend to supervise the handover, but the crew doesn't need my help.

Ellen is there helping the medical team, but in a minute, the radiologists take one patient and the other leaves for surgery.

She comes back into the Emergency Department while the rest of the crew is packing up and finishing their paperwork.

She limps over to me and holds out her clipboard. "Could I get your signature on the supply transfer orders?"

I scribble my signature and then look up at her. "How are you doing?"

She blushes again. "I'm good. How are you? Did you get your rental yet?"

"Yeah, I got it. I'm moving in at the end of the week."

She smiles at me. "You look good. You look more alive—less like a cadaver."

I laugh—and I feel my cheeks burning. "I deserved that."

"At least you can laugh. I need to call you later about arrangements for the next barbecue. What time would be good when you aren't too busy?"

I make a face. "Are you serious? You were married to the former Fire Chief. Don't ask me what time would be good."

Now it's her turn to laugh. "Okay. You got me."

"Just call. If it isn't a good time, I'll hang up on you. Simple."

She won't stop blushing. She makes me feel so much better.

I don't have to act any particular way. I don't have to act sad about Naomi because Ellen already knows I am. I have nothing to prove to her.

She leaves to go back to work, the crew finishes packing up, and we ride back to the firehouse.

I help the crew restock and then Caleb shows me something wrong with one of the lockers on the side of the rescue truck.

Something must have hit the lock too hard. The catch bent and now he has to yank it extra hard to open it and slam it extra hard to shut it.

Carter comes over to take a look, too.

"I'll have to write this up," I tell them. "The truck will have to go in for maintenance to fix it, which means the Department will have to send us a loaner truck to use while ours is out of service."

"Do you have to?" Caleb asks. "It isn't that bad. Can't we just use it the way it is?"

"This is one of the critical vehicle functions," Carter tells him. "The truck has to go in the very first time one of the locks malfunctions the same way we would have to send it in right away if the windshield got broken."

Caleb rolls his eyes. "That's stupid."

"It will take time for the department to get around to assigning us a replacement truck anyway," I add. "We'll be stuck with it like this for a few more days...."

"Or it could be weeks," Carter corrects.

I find myself laughing again, so I take myself off to my office.

I'm just about to walk into it when Vince comes out of the break-room. Don't ask me what he's doing in there when the rest of the crew is all downstairs restocking after the call.

I find out what he's doing here the minute he opens his mouth. "What the hell are you doing moving in on Ellen?" he snaps.

I stumble back in shock, first at his tone and second that he could think I was doing anything with Ellen. "Um....what are you talking about?" I ask.

"I saw you at the hospital! You were both making eyes at each other. I'm not stupid. I've been trying to get her to go out with me for weeks."

I pretend to look right and left. "Does that have anything to do with me?"

"It does if you're moving in on her in my place. What are you trying to pull? You don't just get to do that because you're the boss, so don't even think about pulling rank on me."

"I'm not pulling rank on you because nothing is going on between me and Ellen. She's been helping me get over Naomi and Amelia. That's all...."

"Then why are you two making googy eyes at each other in the ED?!" His voice starts to rise. "I saw you at her house the other day! Don't even bother to deny it!"

My jaw drops. "How do you know about that?"

He jabs his finger in my face. "See?! I know you were there because I saw you. I went over there to check on her and bring her dinner that I made for her. I saw her pull up in her car and take you inside."

I turn away and head for my office. I'm not having this conversation with him. I can only bring myself to answer him at all by snapping over my shoulder at him.

"Believe it or not, pal, that happened less than ten minutes after I just watched Naomi code in her hospital bed. I was a mess. Ellen happened to be there and she took me out of the hospital because I was a wreck. She took me to her house to help me calm down."

He follows talking in my ear the whole time. "I don't believe you. You were making a move on her."

I snort. "Are you really going to stand there and tell me I made a move on Ellen the very minute my wife just dropped dead in front of my eyes?"

He follows me all the way into my office. I'm just planning to lay the smackdown on him the minute we get into a private, enclosed space.

I stop dead in my tracks when I discover Keith and Danny Brewer waiting for me in my office. I don't know why they're here, but I don't like the expressions on their faces at all.

Vince doesn't see Keith and Danny in time. He actually collides with me from behind when I stop too suddenly. He has to walk around me before he sees what I'm staring at.

Keith glares at both of us. "Is there a problem here?"

I try to wave it away. "Not at all. Just a little difference of opinion."

"We heard every word." Keith turns to Vince. "You better not be up here making Duke's life difficult after the shit he's just been going through. I swear, if I find you you're causing trouble, they will never find the missing pieces of what's left of you."

"I know what I saw!" Vince blurts out.

"What happens between Duke and Ellen is none of your business, chump," Danny cuts in. "Do your job. You don't get paid to turn the firehouse into a goddamn soap opera."

I cringe at his tone. Danny is always so kind and easy-going. I've never heard him speak this harshly to anyone.

I don't have to give Vince a smackdown. These two are doing it a hundred times worse than I ever could.

Keith takes a threatening step toward Vince. "Let's just be real clear right up front, man, just in case this wasn't glaringly obvious from the beginning. Duke has our unwavering support—in everything he does. His wife is barely cold so it isn't likely that he would get interested in another woman just a few days later—but even if he did, even if there was something going on between him and Ellen, he would have our full support on that, too."

"Damn straight," Danny chimes in. "I can't think of anyone better for her than Duke. He would be a hell of a lot better for her than *you.*" Danny sneers the last word and shoots his hard eyes down Vince's body. "Ellen deserves to be happy and Duke is just the man to give it to her—not a spoiled, jealous baby like you."

"It isn't for you two to decide what's best for Ellen!" Vince fires back. "She said she wouldn't go out with me because she wasn't ready to move on."

"She told me the same thing, pal," I interjected. "Neither of us are."

"It isn't for you to decide what's best for Ellen, either," Keith rumbles. "She doesn't need an excuse to turn you down one day and start up with someone else the next. Danny is right. You're acting like a spoiled brat who is having a tantrum because you didn't get your way. Just take it like a man—and you can bet your ass that Danny and I will be watching to make sure you do."

"And just in case you didn't hear it the first time," Danny cuts in, "if you don't think we have anything to say about what's best for Ellen, think again. We will always look out for Ellen—always. If she told you no, then that's the last word. Now you back off. The reason doesn't mean shit to us. If we find out you're harassing her or giving her a hard time about going out with someone else, you'll be hearing from us—and not in a nice way. Got that?"

Vince glares at them, but of course he doesn't have an answer. He storms out of the room and stomps off down the stairs. He really is a toddler.

I let out a shaky breath as soon as he leaves. "Thanks, fellas," I croak.

Keith shoots me a flinty glare. "You never have to explain or justify yourself to us—ever. To hell with him—and anyone else who messes with you."

"You deserve to be happy," Danny tells me. "No matter what you do."

I can barely say, "Thanks," again. They leave me alone, but I feel myself shaking.

I sink into my chair, but I can't stop my heart from pounding.

I didn't realize the Brewers' approval would have bothered me when it came to Ellen. I'm not even thinking about her that way, but everyone else seems to be.

Their approval means the world, though. Danny is right. I wouldn't be able to look at her sideways without their approval. They're her family. They're stand-ins for John.

I turn back to my computer and force myself to concentrate, but I can't get that conversation out of my head. Danny actually thinks it's a good idea for me and Ellen to get together.

Keith certainly didn't contradict. What if....?

Chapter 11: Ellen

I force myself to stay sitting down when the front door opens, but my nerves are strained to the breaking point.

Keith walks in first followed by Oakleigh. Danny comes last.

Keith scowls the way he usually does whenever he has to get serious about anything.

Danny frowns much more sternly than usual, too. He always smiles, laughs, and jokes around with everyone. I actually feel scared seeing him like this.

Oakleigh shuffles her feet, knits her fingers together, and looks around at everything other than the three of us.

Danny shuts the door behind him. No one speaks while the three of them sit down with me in the living room.

I'm sitting in an armchair. Keith takes the other.

Oakleigh doesn't know what to do with herself. Danny takes hold of her shoulders and pushes her down on the couch before he sits down next to her.

She's been living with him, Zeke, and Emily for the past week. None of them has said a word to me about how that is going except when Danny came over to pick up some of Oakleigh's clothes, pajamas, and toothbrush.

I really have no idea what to expect from this meeting. I really wouldn't be surprised if Keith and Danny recommend that Oakleigh goes to live with one of them.

I've been mentally preparing myself for that. Now I just have to deal with the nerves of getting through this meeting.

Danny brings a small duffel bag carrying her stuff, but he leaves the bag by the door. The silent implication couldn't be more obvious. There's no guarantee she'll stay here.

Danny takes a deep breath to start things off. "Now…we all know why we're here. Oakleigh and I have talked about her living arrangements." He turns to her. "You've had a week to live away from Ellen. You've seen what it would be like to live with us and you still want to live with her."

Her voice cracks when she blurts out, "Of course I do."

"And I already told you that living with Ellen came with certain rules and conditions," Keith interjects. "You broke those rules by yelling at her, telling her you hate her, and running off. What are we supposed to think from that? How can we let you come back here after we told you that you were on probation and you broke the rules anyway?"

"I only did it because Duke was here!" she counters. "He didn't have to come here. He could have gone anywhere."

"What happens with Duke has nothing to do with this," Keith tells her. "This is about you. Are you telling me that if Josh or Carter or Billy or Caleb lost their wife, you would have a problem with one of them coming over here for a few minutes of rest time before they have to face the nightmare of going home to an empty house? These are the people who helped you and your dad get through your mother's death. How can you be so selfish to deny someone else the same comfort when he needs it?"

She looks away. "But.....we aren't talking about them. We're talking about Duke. He didn't help me and Dad get through that."

"It doesn't matter," Danny cuts in. "None of that matters—and do you know what? It doesn't matter if Ellen does get together with Duke—or if she gets together with anyone else. Duke is a good man and both he and Ellen deserve to be happy. I can't think of anyone better for Ellen to get together with—and if they do, they will get full support from me and Keith—and the rest of the firehouse family—and that includes you. If you want to be a part of this family, you better get on the wagon with the rest of us."

She stares at him and then her eyes dart to me. Her eyes already glisten with tears and her mouth twists in all the wrong shapes. "Are you with him or not?"

I try to wave that away. "That doesn't matter. I can't be your guardian if you think you can dictate terms on my life or any other decision I make about your care. If you live with me, it means you're accepting my decisions about you even if you don't like it. If you can't accept my decisions, then it will be better for you to go live with one of the boys instead."

"And you can bet your boots neither Danny nor I will let you challenge us, either," Keith booms. "You won't boss either of us around—or Leila or Emily—and I can promise you that we will sometimes make decisions that you don't like. We will expect you to do things you don't want to do. You'll have to do them and follow our decisions the same way you would follow your dad—no exceptions. That's just the way it has to be. You know your dad wouldn't put up with that if he was alive and we won't put up with it, either."

Her eyes dart back and forth between all of us. Does she even see us? Did she hear a word Keith just said?

Her eye movements and facial expressions get progressively more frantic.

Danny lowers his voice and softens his tone considerably. He sounds the way he usually does. "Well, sweetie? What do you have to say?"

"I just...." she stammers and twists her fingers in knots. "I just want.....I want....." She falters and then blurts out, "I just want my dad back! I want my dad!"

She bursts into loud sobs, buries her face in her hands, and bolts from the room. She charges away through the house and then we hear her bedroom door slam.

I look away blinking back tears of my own. I want to run out of the room and go put my arms around her, but I can't do that with the guys sitting in front of me.

"What do you want to do?" Keith asks.

"I guess she can move back in again. Maybe we can keep trying to get through to her. Maybe we can just keep moving her out for longer and longer breaks each time she messes up. Maybe that will finally get the message through her head."

He nods. "That's what I was thinking, too. One of these times might be a wake-up call for her."

"Or she might decide she likes it better somewhere else," Danny suggests. He looks up and studies me. "How do you feel about that?"

I try not to sniff too obviously. "It would take some getting used to, but I'm starting to think maybe it will be the best thing for all of us."

"There is a third option," Keith adds. "We could create a three-way custody rotation so she travels between all our houses and spends equal time with all of us—kind of like divorced parents do except that this would be three different houses instead of two."

"Are you serious?!" I gasp. "Wouldn't that make her feel too insecure? She would think she doesn't have a home."

"I think she already feels too insecure as it is. She's completely dependent on you—or she thinks she is. This way, she can see that she'll always be taken care of even if something happens to one of us. It will give her more security—more than she has now. That's why she's acting up—because she feels insecure and she thinks she'll be left alone."

I look away. I never considered this, but it makes so much sense that I can't stop thinking about it, now that he's bringing it up.

He stands up. "Anyway, it's something to think about. We could try it out for a while and see how it goes for all of us. Maybe it will give both of you some much-needed perspective on all of this." He waves to Danny. "Come on, man."

Danny stands up and so do I. I hug them both and walk them to the door.

I'm almost too grateful to thank them for everything they're doing for me. I wouldn't be able to get through any of this without them.

I shut the door behind them, but the hardest part of this still lies in front of me.

I drag my heels to Oakleigh's bedroom and hesitate with my hand on the doorknob. I can hear her crying inside.

She just wants her dad. She wants all of this to go back to the way it was before he died. No one understands that better than I do.

I walk into the room. She lies on her bed sobbing into her pillow. Poor kid.

I fight down tears when I sit on the bed next to her. My throat hurts and so does my face. I've been fighting this down for so long.

I lay my hand on her back and rub. She starts crying harder. "I just want my dad!" she wails. "I just want my dad! Why did he have to die?"

I can't stop the tears from streaking down my cheeks. I would give everything I own to get John back. I would even give my other leg just to see his face one more time.

Without warning, she jerks around on the bed, throws her arms around my waist, and howls in anguish against my stomach.

I keep rubbing her back through it all. I can't answer her questions. I can't give her John back. I can't even deal with my own grief, but that's okay because we share that.

This is the first time she's ever let herself say those words out loud. *I want my dad. Why did he have to die?*

At least she's saying it. At least she's expressing it. Maybe she can find a way to not be so angry about it.

Chapter 12: Duke

My stomach ties up in knots when I pull my pickup into the beach parking lot. It's barbecue day and I'm about to see Ellen again.

I can't let myself think like that. Neither of us is ready for that, especially not me.

Getting back to work has been incredibly good for me—and I see her at the hospital. Everyone has been super supportive and Vince hasn't said a word to me about anything that wasn't job-related.

I don't care if he got his feelings hurt as long as he keeps up his job performance.

The Brewer brothers haven't been taking it easy on him at all. I catch both of them cracking down on him when he needs it and even sometimes when he doesn't need it.

He pulled his head in big time after our unplanned meeting in my office. He knows he made a huge mistake by pissing them off.

The two of them are practically more in charge of the firehouse than I am. No one puts a foot out of line with those two around.

Their involvement makes my life so much easier. I don't even have to think about Vince. I don't have to keep my eye on him. They do it for me and they bring the hammer down at the earliest opportunity.

He behaves himself to stay on their good side more than on mine. I want to laugh when I think about it, but I don't even have to think about it enough to do that much.

I have my own things to worry about when I get out of the truck and heft my shopping bags from behind the seat.

I brought fireworks again this time—and a few big water cannons from the toy store. No one seems to have thought of that even though we're right here next to an enormous water source.

I head down to the beach to find almost everyone already there. The on-duty crew made it here just before me. They're all settling in.

For the first time since I've been working in Howe, Oakleigh actually stands with the group instead of going off to sit by herself in the dunes.

She hangs especially close to Ellen. Oakleigh keeps looking around at everyone and cringing like she wants to disappear.

Everyone else treats her presence as something normal, so I do the same thing. I try to avoid her and I also avoid Ellen even though I don't want to.

I catch her making eye contact with me and immediately looking away to go back to her conversations.

We wouldn't normally avoid talking to each other at these events, but it doesn't seem appropriate anymore—not after everyone keeps dropping hints about us.

I put my stuff on the picnic table. I plan to just leave the water cannons in the bag and let the kids discover them on their own, but it doesn't work out that way.

Zeke Montgomery comes right up to me and pulls open the bag of firecrackers—and then his eyes fall out of their sockets when he sees the water cannons. "Um.....what are those?"

"They're giant water guns." I pull one out and show it to him. "You open it here, hold it underwater until it fills up, and then you close the port, pump the handle, and shoot." I catch his eye and hold the gun out to him. "Do you want to try it?"

"You mean....who did you bring this for?"

"For you, of course. You and the other kids."

He shoots a sidelong glance at Danny. "Maybe I should ask first."

"Why? You can't hurt anyone. It's just water." I get a crazy idea and pull the gun back toward myself. "I'll keep this one. You better arm yourself before I get there or you're gonna get wet."

I kick off my shoes and take off running down the beach. I get to the water's edge, wade in up to my shins, and plunge the gun underwater.

It starts bubbling as the magazine fills. I glance over my shoulder and giggle when I see Zeke wrestling another gun out of the bag.

A bunch of other kids go over there in time to see what he's doing. I hear their voices rising from here.

I have to fight down nervous laughter when I see them running toward the water, each kid carrying a weapon—an empty weapon.

I lunge out of the surf, cram the stopper back into the magazine, pump my cannon, and open fire on the whole pack of kids.

They shriek and scatter. None of them dares to come near the water with me blocking the way.

I burst into maniacal laughter while I bombard them all and soak their clothes. I try to concentrate on Zeke, but I get distracted when some of the kids break through to the waves.

I try to hit them, too, but my gun runs out of water just then. I have to go back to reload.

It's all on after that. The kids get their weapons loaded and turn them on me and each other.

I squat down in the shallow water to refill my magazine. A bunch of kids, including Zeke, take advantage of the moment to come up behind me and bombard my head and back with water.

They saturate my clothes. I'm even wearing my uniform because I'm still on duty.

There's nothing I can do but crouch here and take it until I refill my own weapon.

I plug the hole, stand up, turn around, and fire. The kids run around screaming and drenching each other. I get Zeke back and plaster a bunch of other kids.

We're running around laughing. I'm getting winded from running so much.....and then I see it.

I stop dead in my tracks staring down the beach. I don't even feel it when multiple sprays hit me from behind.

The beach.

The memory of that day comes rushing back. My first date with Naomi was a firehouse barbecue. We went for a walk down this beach.

We talked about having kids together. We told each other our darkest secrets.....and then we did it for the first time on the beach.

We went swimming in the waves and did it in the water.

What the hell am I doing running around like a kid having a water fight after what happened to her?

I want to throw the gun away. I want to get it as far out of my hands as possible, but I can't do that here—not without throwing it in the ocean.

Zeke runs up to me, grabs my arm by the elbow for a split second, gives me a slight tug, and yells out in a breathless rush, "Come on, Duke!" before he runs off into the battle.

I barely see him or feel him. I can't do this. I shouldn't even be here. I shouldn't have come to this barbecue.......

If I don't come to this barbecue because of what happened between me and Naomi at the beach—if that's the reason I stay away—then I would never come to anymore barbecues ever again.

I couldn't do that. I'm the Fire Chief. I have to come.

I don't have to come. I could stay in my office like Ebenezer Scrouge while everyone else enjoys being the close-knit family John Brewer made them.

I couldn't do that.

Some part of me knows I'm not dishonoring Naomi's and Amelia's memories by coming to the barbecues and even enjoying myself.

I'm not doing anything wrong by having a life and even laughing at things I find funny or enjoyable.

I stand frozen in time staring down the beach. I can't move. I can't think. I can't hear anything.

I just stand here letting the memory take over. I never want to forget that day....just like I don't want to forget the feeling of my lips on Amelia's baby-soft scalp.....just like I don't want to forget her smell.....and Naomi's smell.....

I don't want to forget the feeling of Naomi on my lap right over there beyond those trees.

There are so many of those moments I want to remember. I want my life to become an eternal memory capsule to them and the people who made my life such a joy.

I can't do that. I know I have to move on, but I don't have to do it now.

Out of nowhere, Ellen appears at my side and lays her hand on my shoulder. "Are you okay?" she asks in a soft undertone.

I hear her, but I can't respond. The memories hold too much power over me.

Of course it had to be her. She's the only one who can break through this shell around me.

She doesn't wait for me to respond. She pulls the water gun out of my hand, takes hold of my elbow the way Zeke did, and she doesn't let go.

She leads me back over to the barbecue. "Come over here," she murmurs.

I stumble under her guidance back to where the rest of the adults stand around talking. She drops the water gun on the picnic table as we pass.

I notice Oakleigh walking off toward the parking lot. I wouldn't have expected Ellen to say anything to me or even pay attention to me as long as Oakleigh was around.

I hope Oakleigh and Ellen won't have any more problems because of me—especially not because Ellen just pulled me out of that memory.

Then again, Oakleigh could be on her way to the parking lot to go to the bathroom. How should I know?

Ellen steers me into the circle, pulls a bottle of juice out of one of the coolers, and shoves it into my hands.

She leaves me there while she goes to the picnic table and starts making a plate of food for me. She visits the grill, gets something from Danny, and then brings the plate back to me.

The crew is talking about their latest training session. They had to practice taking blood sugar tests by pricking their fingers, drawing a drop of blood, and testing it.

I catch Keith, Carter, and plenty of others casting questioning glances in my direction while the crew shoots remarks and jokes back and forth.

I barely hear them. I twist the cap off my drink and then start eating the food Ellen gave me. She goes back to the picnic table, gets a plate of her own, comes back to stand next to me, and starts eating.

Everything she does and everything we do is so casual and normal. All of this is normal and yet it means everything.

Eating with her here is the same as eating on the front porch of my house. It's so unbelievably normal.

The inevitable gravity of such a normal, ordinary, mundane activity pulls me along with it. I wind up doing it instead of thinking myself into a paralysis about it.

Sometimes I wonder if Ellen even knows what a godsend she is, but she must know because she went through it all when she lost John.

She's doing for me what she would have needed someone to do for her back then.

All of this comes so naturally to her and yet it's so meaningful and perfect. I get another, almost crushing surge of gratitude that someone around here knows enough to intervene when I need her to.

Oakleigh comes back after a while. She stands next to Ellen in the circle and listens to the adults talk, but after a while, Oakleigh loses interest and turns away.

The kids are still waging the Battle of the Bulge out on the sand. They don't seem to be getting tired at all or losing interest. It looks like the water guns are a hit.

Oakleigh goes to the picnic table to get something to eat. She's standing there when Zeke comes over panting, grinning, and gasping out a few words before he runs off.

Oakleigh tries to get interested in the food again, but her attention always migrates back to the other kids.

I don't know what she was like before John's death, but she sure looks sad that she can't join the others in their games.

Without warning, she snatches my old water gun off the table and takes off running for the water.

The other kids are too busy attacking each other to intervene. She gets hit with stray spray from the other kids' battles before she gets her weapon filled and stands up.

She turns around, narrows her eyes at her enemies, and unloads. In a few minutes, she's running around all over the place and yelling with the best of them.

I can't even be glad that I gave her this moment. I can't even be glad that I gave myself this moment.

I keep my back to the kids and don't watch. I go through the motions of eating my food, drinking my drink, and answering questions when anyone asks me.

That's the most I'm capable of at the moment.

I need to change out of my wet uniform. I wait an appropriate amount of time—just long enough so that everyone in the circle can see that I'm not in any danger of losing my mind.

Ellen stands next to me the whole time. She eats her food, drinks her drink, and even participates in the conversation, but she never says a word to me.

None of that matters. When the time comes, I head up to my truck, take out a clean uniform, and change in the bathroom.

I stash the wet uniform in the back of the truck before I head back down to the beach.

I'm just crossing the parking lot when I catch another glimpse of the beach behind the curved headland of trees.

That's the beach where I went for a walk with Naomi. That's the beach where it all started.

I can't turn away this time and I don't want to. Ellen isn't here to pull me out of it and I don't want her to.

I just want to remember—just once.

I know it won't be more than once, but it somehow seems important that I remember it now.

I pull on my jacket and send Keith a text telling him I'm going for a walk. I tell him I'll see him and the crew back at the firehouse.

He texts back a thumbs-up emoji. What a great guy he is. He said I never had to explain or justify anything to him and he damn well meant it.

I slip away to the other side of the beach—the side where no one can see me.

I disappear into the memory and let it take me back to that day. Just for now, just for a few minutes, I can pretend like that day never ended.

Naomi and I wouldn't have gotten Amelia if that day never ended. It did end and it turned into something even more wonderful.

This beach means so many things to me now. It means the entirety of my relationship with them. It means all the beautiful, heartwarming moments that made our time so precious.

They were precious because they were limited.

I don't cry because of the way they ended. I cry because they happened at all.

I cry because I had the privilege of being there.

I cry for the searing brand of love they left on my life. I'll never be the same after that and I don't want to be.

I want to be a man who is capable of that kind of love. I never want to lose that—not ever.

Chapter 13: Ellen

I rub the towel over Oakleigh's hair and down her body. She stands shivering in front of me with her hair soaked. Her lips don't work right and her teeth chatter.

I try not to make a big deal about her playing with the other kids at the barbecue. This is the first time she let herself do that in a long time.

I don't make a big deal about her getting her clothes wet, either. I don't really know what to say good or bad, so I wind up saying nothing.

I get her as dry as possible and lift her clean, warm, dry T-shirt to pull it over her head.

I kneel down in front of her so she can slip her feet into her dry sweatpants.

"You're gonna go stay with Keith and Leila for a little while," I tell her.

"Why?" she stammers.

"We decided the other night after you came home from Danny's. We think it will be better if you rotate between all three of us. That way, you'll start to see that all three of us are responsible for taking care of you. Then you'll understand that you won't be alone or in trouble if something happens to one of us."

"Why can't I stay with you?" she falters.

I have to smile at her. "You will be staying with me. You'll be staying with all three of us. We'll see each other all the time. This doesn't mean you did anything wrong. We're doing this because we want to help you. You said you were scared that something would happen to me and you would be left alone. We want to help you overcome that fear by giving you a wider base of support if you understand what I mean. You have a lot of people taking care of you—not just me."

She doesn't stop me when I sit her down on her bed and put her socks on for her. I leave the shoes for her to do.

Her shivering subsides when she gets her clothes on. I pull a heavy sweater over her head and then put a jacket on her. She'll need them when she goes to Keith's anyway. She might as well wear them there instead of putting them in her bag.

I go through her room and the bathroom packing up the stuff she'll need to stay at his house.

I get distracted by the job and don't notice her watching me.

"Ellen?" she asks.

"Yeah?" I ask over my shoulder.

"Do you ever wish you didn't have me to take care of?"

I freeze at those words. It takes me what feels like a long time to work up the courage to turn around and face her.

I have to, though. I go over to the bed and sit down next to her. I find it hard to look at her, so I stare at the floor.

"I don't wish I didn't have you to take care of," I murmur. "Sometimes I wonder if me taking care of you is making it harder for you—like maybe I'm the one who is keeping you stuck in remembering your dad instead of you being able to move on. I don't know. Maybe we're both doing that to each other. Maybe I'm the worst thing for you. I know you don't think that. I know you love me as much as ever and I love you, but maybe that's the problem. Maybe we're too close and we both share too much of the same pain. Maybe you moving between all three houses will be the best thing for both of us. I wish it wasn't. I wish I could believe that keeping you here was the best thing for you....because I don't want to let you go—not ever."

My throat constricts and my eyes overflow with tears. I have to look at her.

I really do love her like my own daughter. Maybe that's the problem.

I can't stand the way she's looking at me. I pull her into a hug and kiss her on top of the head.

I push her back right away and sniff back tears. I can't let this turn into a mushy, painful, agonizing farewell.

I want this to become routine and ordinary. I want this whole experiment of her moving between all three houses to become a regular part of her life.

"Let's pack up the rest of your stuff," I tell her. "Keith will be here in a few minutes."

I stand up and start gathering her things into the duffel bag she brought back from Danny's. The week she spent with Danny's family is the perfect segue into her spending the same amount of time with Keith before she comes back to me.

I'm just zipping up her bag when I hear Keith knock on the front door. Oakleigh is still rummaging around in her chest of drawers when I go out to the living room to let him in.

He gives me one of his hard looks. "How is she doing with it all?"

I nod. "I think she's okay with it. We just talked about it. She seems to understand that this might be for the best."

He puffs out his cheeks and his expression softens. "Phew! I was bracing myself for another hysterical knockdown-dragout fight to haul her kicking and screaming out of the house."

I smile at him. "Not at all. She seems fine."

"So where is she?" He looks around. "Let's get this done."

I yell up the hall to Oakleigh's bedroom. "Oakleigh—come on! Keith is here! It's time to go!"

"I can't find my watch!" she yells back. "It isn't here!"

"You don't need it!" Keith hollers. "You can get it later."

"I need it for school!" Her voice rises to a shriek. "I can't go back to school without it!"

Now it's my turn to give Keith a look. He stays in the living room while I go to her room to straighten out this latest catastrophe.

She stands at her dresser pawing through mountains of crap piled on top of it. She keeps pulling open the same drawers over and over again and not finding the watch.

"Where was the last place you know you had it?" I ask.

"I had it at the beach!" she cries. "I was wearing it when I used the water gun on the other kids. I took my watch off because it isn't waterproof and I didn't want to wreck it."

"Where did you put it?"

"I put it in my pocket!" Her hand flies to her hip. "I swear I wanted to keep it safe! That's the only reason I took it off!"

I make a quick search of the room and then check the pocket of the wet pants I just took off her.

"It isn't here. You must have dropped it at the beach," I tell her. "Go out to the living room. It's time for you to go to Keith's house. I'll keep searching for it, and if I don't find it, I'll go back to the beach and look for it there."

She looks up at me. "You aren't mad? I promise I didn't mean to lose it."

"No, sweetie, I'm not mad. I'm sure you took all the right steps to keep it safe. We'll find it, and even if we don't, it's just a thing. It isn't that important. Now come on. Keith is waiting for you."

I walk her out to the living room and hand her over to Keith. She won't leave until I make her numerous promises that I'll find the watch no matter what.

Keith keeps giving me that look behind her back until I finally push her out the door. I wait until he drives off with her in his truck.

I go over her room with a fine-toothed comb and still don't find the watch. I go through every pocket of the clothes she was wearing at the beach. She must have dropped it there without realizing.

Chapter 14: Ellen

I get in the car and drive out to the beach, but I still don't find Oakleigh's watch no matter how much I search in the sand, around the picnic table, near the waves, in the bathrooms, and everywhere else I know Oakleigh was today.

I go back and forth multiple times between the picnic table and the parking lot bathroom, but I still don't find it.

I give up and head for my car to leave. I must have missed something.

I'm just taking out my keys to go home when Duke steps out of the trees on the other side of the parking lot.

I stare at him for a minute before I realize he must have been out here the whole time. He never left the barbecue—or rather, he never left the beach after he left the barbecue.

He went to change his clothes and he didn't come back. He must have been walking around on the beach in a trance this whole time.

His eyes dart away when he sees that it's me. He crosses the parking lot to me, but he keeps his gaze averted.

"Hi," he murmurs.

"Hi," I greet him. "Are you okay? You didn't come back to the barbecue. Don't worry. I wasn't concerned. I just thought you would be back at work by now." I look around at the empty parking lot. "Where's your truck?"

"Keith took it back to the firehouse. I texted him to ask him to take over so I could spend some time out here by myself." He squints toward the trees from which he just emerged. "Naomi and I had our first date here."

"I remember." I find myself smirking at him. "I seem to recall you two vanishing off the map that day. Did this have something to do with that?"

He sees me grinning at him and looks away, but his lips still twitch to stop himself from smiling. "Something like that."

I busy myself unlocking my car. "John and I hooked up here the first time, too."

His head shoots up. "Really?"

"I mean...we didn't hook up here. We started kissing here and he asked me to come back to his house.....for the first time." I feel my cheeks burning. "I shouldn't even be telling you this. Just forget I said anything."

He won't stop staring at me. "That's okay. I want to know."

I look away. "There's nothing more to tell. Oakleigh was spending the night at some other kids' house, so we went back to their house. End of story."

"Did you stay together after that? Was that really the end of the story?"

"Oh, no! Nothing as simple or straightforward as that." I find myself laughing more out of nerves than anything else. "It could never be that simple or straightforward where I'm concerned."

"So what happened?"

"I got injured....and then I spent a long time in rehab.....and then I got all weird about our relationship because I had a disabled leg.....and he had to talk some sense into me and make me realize that it didn't make me any less attractive just because my leg was screwed up."

He stares at me with huge eyes. "It doesn't."

I look away again. The way he's looking at me makes me think.....Is he really thinking of me like that?

I should drive away right now. I don't want to get involved with Duke Broebeck.... except that I do.

He's one of the most attractive men at the firehouse. He's older, more mature, more responsible.......just like John.

Duke is nothing like John, though. Duke is steadier, more solid. John was fiery in a powerful, unmovable kind of way.

Duke doesn't have John's solidity, either in his build or in his personality, but Duke is just as appealing. He's almost irresistible—almost.

He won't stop staring at me. He doesn't avert his gaze now. "Did Oakleigh have a problem with you when you and John got together?" he asks.

"Oh, no!" I burst out laughing again and find myself blushing. "She practically pushed us together. She wanted us to get together long before anything actually happened between us. She got stranded at school once. Her carpool forgot to pick her up and John and the boys were busy on a call. The school couldn't get in touch with any of them, so the vice-principal called the firehouse. I was the only one there, so I wound up taking the call. Then I picked her up and took her home until John came home from work. Oakleigh got this crazy idea about us being together and she wouldn't let it go. She hounded him for months to come visit me in rehab even though he already was visiting me in rehab. She nagged him to invite me over for dinner....and a bunch of other stuff. She didn't have a problem with him getting together with me."

He blinks at me in wonder. "Wow. That sounds amazing."

I really wish he would stop looking at me like that. "It wasn't amazing. It was messy....and awkward.....and it took me way too long to accept that I could have a relationship with him and be disabled at the same time. I didn't really accept it until I got the job at the hospital. I had to feel like I could still do my job before I let myself really have a relationship with him."

He stares at me long after I finish talking. Does he even realize I stopped talking?

He finally looks away across the parking lot—toward the trees. No one remembers that the way I do.

I'm fully prepared to end the conversation there, but right then, he leans back against the car like he plans to stay here for a while.

He keeps gazing across the parking lot toward the trees. He's a million miles away—or so I think.

"Oakleigh thinks there's something going on between us," he murmurs.

I turn bright red again, but he isn't looking at me, thank Heaven. "I know."

"I mean, it seems like a lot of people think that."

I have to gulp to get my throat working. Does Duke know what Danny said about me getting together with Duke?

"I know," I choke.

"Everything in my rational mind tells me my wife is barely in the ground and whatever this is going on between you and me has nothing to do with that......" He looks over at me and our eyes lock. "But maybe it does."

Now it's my turn to blink at him. Is he really suggesting what I think he's suggesting?

Before I can even think about what that would mean, he leans in and kisses me. He does it lightly, but he doesn't just give me a light peck and move off.

He lingers there on my lips....kissing gently.....just to test the waters.

I stare at his hard crystal eyes staring straight back at me from inches away.

He trails off my lips and straightens up. "I don't know why I did that," he murmurs, "except that something about it feels right."

I force myself to look away. "I'm not ready for that."

"Neither am I.....and yet I still seem to be doing it."

He cups my cheek in one hand and turns me around to face him. His eyes won't let me go.

"Maybe it's right," he murmurs. "Maybe it makes a bizarre kind of sense."

I can't stop staring at him. He doesn't kiss me again. He just stands there with his hand on my cheek.

My mind reels when I finally bring myself to comprehend that he kissed me. He's actually doing this.

Danny's words come back to me. He actually thinks this is a good idea. He actually thinks it would be a good thing for me to get together with Duke.

There does seem to be a kind of symmetry about all of this. John was Fire Chief. He died under the worst, most tragic circumstances possible.

Now Duke is Fire Chief. His wife just died under the worst most tragic circumstances possible.

Could it be that all these twists of fate have been steering me and Duke together? They certainly seem to be.

I see it all in his eyes. He's magnetic, powerful, and unbelievably attractive. His heart is beyond pure. I never thought I would ever meet a man with a heart as pure as John's.

Now Duke is standing right here in front of me. He doesn't even have to kiss me a second time.

He isn't ready and I'm not ready, but maybe that's kind of the point, isn't it?

Maybe neither of us will ever be ready. Maybe we don't need to be because we're both in the same place with not being ready.

His eyes radiate so many unspoken meanings. I see and understand so many things when I look at him. I actually see myself.

I don't have to explain anything to him because he already knows. He knows everything about me and I know everything about him. We're mirrors of each other.

He passes his thumbs up and down my cheeks in such a gentle stroking motion. It's the most tender movement imaginable, but it speaks volumes. Nothing will ever be the same between us.

Neither of us has to say the words. It's already done.

I don't know how or where or even if we decided to change something, but it does. He lets go of my face, leans in, and we both start kissing madly, passionately, ravenously.

His arms close around my waist and lift me off the ground to meet his mouth. I hug him around the neck as tightly as I can.

I need to kiss him as deeply as possible. I don't know how long this will last. This moment might pass in a minute and disappear into nothing.

I have to kiss him with everything I have now while I have the chance.

He kisses differently and tastes differently from John, but I actually love the fact that Duke is different. He's a different person. I don't want him to be the same. I don't want him to be John.

In that moment, another thought comes to my mind. I don't want John. I'm kissing Duke. I want Duke.

Just thinking that makes me attack him even harder. I want him. I want to get him.

John has been dead for over a year. What am I waiting for? I have a strong, kind, good-hearted man right in front of me—right here in my arms.

I want Duke. I don't even care if I'm a rebound for him after Naomi's death. I just want him.

He senses the change and comes at me just as hard. His body tenses with muscle. He's so much taller than John and no less chiseled.

Duke falls back against the car with me draped over him while we both inhale each other to the ends of the Earth. I don't want this to end.

My fingers thread into his hair and down to his neck. I wish I could touch more of him, but his shoulders get in the way.

All at once, he spins around, rolls over on the car, and pins me against it under his weight. He lunges in to kiss me twice as hard and then his mouth tears away from me. His hot breath scorches into my mouth and he pants heavily with every contraction in his body.

He grinds into my pelvis and his fingertips rake down my sides to my hips. He scoops both hands under my ass to pull me up the car, but he doesn't draw my legs apart.

His body ripples down me in a delicious, suggestive wave to his hard package digging between my thighs. My slit aches with juicy pulsations when I think about straddling him and taking him into my swollen channel.

Chapter 15: Ellen

For some cosmic reason written in time, Duke eases off me, but he doesn't stop kissing me. He straightens up just enough to lower my feet to the ground, but he doesn't break away from my mouth.

I don't want to let him go. I keep my arms strapped around his neck and swirl my tongue around his in so many luscious rings. His tongue dances with mine.

I feel that tongue between my legs right now as if he's licking me to screaming rapture. I get hotter, wetter, and actually moan in desire when I think about all the things his tongue can do.

He keeps stroking my hair, squeezing the back of my neck to steer my mouth into his, and rubbing down my sides to grip my hips.

He doesn't lean me against the car a second time. He just stands there kissing me...until the inevitable moment when he really does straighten up.

He keeps passing his soft, gentle thumb up and down my cheeks while he gazes into my eyes.

I don't see a trace of grief or doubt when I look back at him like that. A small smile plays on his lips. It isn't even a sad smile.

It's the smile of someone who wants so much more and is okay with knowing he'll probably walk away without it. It's the smile of a man who knows what he wants and still expects nothing.

I don't know what to think or say. I can't believe I actually kissed him like that—and he kissed me.

His eyes don't waver. He doesn't hide from what we just did.

"You should probably get going," he murmurs. "Oakleigh is probably wondering where you are."

I shudder and the spell dissolves. I shake my head trying to clear my thoughts.

He takes that as a signal to lower his hand from my face, but he doesn't remove it completely. He drops it to rest on my shoulder.

He only lets it sit there casually—almost as if he doesn't realize it's even there.

It means something, though. That hand lays a claim on me. He wants more. He wants a lot more. He just doesn't allow himself to go that far.

"She's....she's staying with Keith," I blurt out. "She isn't staying at my house...I mean the house....I mean...." I flounder for a way to explain myself. "We decided...." I flap my hands in confusion. "It's complicated.....but she isn't waiting for me. She doesn't even know I'm here....I mean...she does, but she doesn't know what this is all about.....I mean....you know....."

He frowns. "Why are you here, then? Did you come out here to think about John?"

"No, no!" I hear myself talking way too fast. "She lost her watch. She thought she dropped it at the beach. So I said I would come out here and look for it, but it isn't here, either. I don't know. It doesn't matter."

I have to come up with something to say. Just don't ask me what that will be. I see myself babbling and putting my foot in my mouth like a moron.

"How are you getting back to the firehouse?" I finally ask.

"I guess I'll just walk, but it's getting too late now. I suppose I can just walk home."

I look up. "Home? I thought you moved out."

"I mean to my new rental."

"Oh. Well, do you want a ride?"

He blinks at me and then at the car. "Okay. Thanks."

I unlock the door for him and he gets into the passenger seat. I back out of the beach parking lot and start driving. He gives me directions.

I drive to an apartment complex on the far opposite side of Howe. He would have been walking a long way to get back to his rental.

"This is it," he tells me. "Thank you for the ride."

"Sure. No problem." I look up at him…and see him looking at me that way.

He bends across the seat and kisses me again—madly. He devours my mouth and his tongue lights me on fire.

It's a good thing I'm going to be driving straight home after this. I wouldn't be able to function otherwise.

That kiss goes on and on and on. I could attack him right here in the seat, but that wouldn't be appropriate for a respectable widow like me.

My being revolts against that. I don't want to be a respectable widow. I want to be a vibrant woman with her whole life in front of her.

I don't know if I could ever have that with Duke, but I want to try.

I keep waiting for the moment when he gets out of the car. He'll stop kissing me any second now. Then all of this will come to a screeching halt.

Maybe that's for the best.

The moment eventually comes. He drifts off my mouth with another sultry hot exhalation of strained breath through his nose.

He sits up, unbuckles his seatbelt, opens the door, puts one leg outside, and glances back at me over his shoulder. "Thanks again for the ride."

I call after him. "Have a good night."

He starts to turn his head, stops, and then comes back inside the car. He twists around in his seat, picks something up from the floor behind the driver's seat, and hands me Oakleigh's watch. "She must have dropped it in here."

"Thanks!" I exclaim. "You're a hero!"

He smirks and blushes. He looks absolutely drop-dead gorgeous when he blushes like that. "Hardly."

He turns away to leave...and stops again.

He stares through the windshield for a split second, dives for me, and nails me all the way back against the seat with an all-consuming, feral kiss.

At the same time, his hand closes around my breast through my blouse. He massages it hard and pinches to tease my nipple through my shirt.

I moan and then yelp as waves of passion take me over. I try to steady myself and wind up grabbing his shoulder.

That grasp feels half like pushing him away and half like pulling him closer. I don't know what to do with all this sensation coursing through my veins.

His hand and mouth make me unbearably hot, wet, and aching between my legs. I want to run away from all the desire taking me over right now.

He reads my mind, lets go of my breast, and plunges his hand between my legs. In seconds, he squeezes me tight through my pants and starts massaging me to epic madness.

I scream into his mouth, and without warning, I blast into a torrential climax that explodes my world apart.

This is the first time I've had an orgasm since John died. I can't handle it. I jerk and convulse on the seat trying to throw myself back against it and throw myself into his hand at the same time.

I cascade into an avalanche of cosmic explosions. I can't stop sobbing, whimpering, and roaring into Duke's mouth as the waves crash over me. What the hell is happening to me?

He breaks off my mouth, crams his forehead against mine, and bares his teeth in a husky snarl while he wrings the last brutal surges from my shattered body.

"Come inside," he rasps. "Come inside and be with me."

I can only whine in pathetic moans. He leaves my body feeling electric and storm-tossed.

"I want you," he whispers under his breath. "I need you. Come inside. You know we both need this."

I can't look into his burning eyes. They hold me spellbound from inches away. "I don't think I can do this!" I choke.

"I don't, either," he murmurs. "I don't know what this is, but I have to do it. I have to have you. I don't know why. It doesn't make any sense. I only know I need you."

Like magic, his hand clamps on my breast again, and this time, he doesn't let go. He twists and pinches my nipple harder through my blouse and bra.

He makes me yelp again and then sob in epic desire. He's right. I need this. I need it like my life depends on it.

"Give it to me," he snarls. "Give yourself to me."

I need him so bad I feel like I'm going to cry, but he doesn't let me go. He keeps massaging my breast while I squirm in an agony of desire on the seat.

I wouldn't be able to stop now, but he does it for me. He breaks off and turns away too fast. I'm still sitting there reeling on the driver's seat. I don't even think to turn off the motor.

He gets out of the car. He doesn't ask permission when he shuts the passenger door, walks around the car to the driver's side, opens my door, and leans across me.

My every nerve stretches to the breaking point when he brushes against me. The energy coming from him blows my world apart.

He unfastens my seatbelt, turns the keys in the ignition to shut off the motor, removes the keys, and takes my hand to pull me out of the car.

Chapter 16: Ellen

I get out of my car in a daze. Duke grabs my purse, shuts the door, and puts my keys in my bag before he takes my hand again.

I can't think when he leads me inside his apartment. He doesn't let go of my hand when he unlocks the door with his other hand.

The door shuts with a kind of monumental finality. I'm alone with him in his apartment with the door shut.

The apartment is really nice. It's an upscale, modernistic, two-bedroom apartment with a big sliding door leading onto a balcony overlooking the parking lot.

The interior follows a modernistic white and grey color scheme with a minimalist open-plan kitchen, grey square leather furniture in the living room, glass coffee and side tables, and a large flat-screen TV on the wall.

Duke puts my handbag on a table by the door and comes toward me very, very slowly. There's no question about what he wants or why I'm here.

He takes hold of my jacket....and tugs it off my shoulder. Everything he does sets my nerves alight. He's going to undress me....and then.....

He takes my jacket off and tosses it on the kitchen counter. His eyes tell me in no uncertain terms what he's about to do.

I tremble in front of him. I'm not so much scared of what he's going to do. I'm more scared of myself.

I don't know why. It isn't like I don't know enough about what's going to happen.

I'm scared of my own feelings. I'm scared of how much I want this.

I'm scared that I'm about to do it with another man for the first time since John died.

I can't even wrap my mind around the irony that the man I'm about to do it with is the Fire Chief who replaced my dead husband. This has to be the universe's idea of a joke.

It might be a good joke or it might be a bad joke. I can't think about it when Duke tears away from my mouth, drops on his knees, pulls my pants down in one quick movement, and plunges between my legs.

He takes me so much by surprise that I scream out—and then the heat from his mouth dissolves all the barriers holding me back.

I try to spread my legs, miss my balance, and fall against the wall behind me, but there's no stopping him.

He burrows between my thighs prying my legs apart.

I have to balance on my brace to hold myself up, but he's escalating too fast for me to correct in time.

He grabs my good leg, lifts it by the knee, and I almost topple again before he catches me.

He holds me there while he devours me in greedy mouthfuls. The orgasm he gave me in the car ignites all over again. I can't slow down.

His mouth snatches me out of this world and spirals me into another whirlwind tempest of pleasure and churning passion.

I grab at his hair, claw at his shoulders, and try to hold onto the wall at the same time. I can't keep my balance, but he holds me in position so I don't fall.

This feeling of tumbling through open space sends me reeling into another climax even more bone-crushingly insane than the last one.

I spike out of my mind, and like something out of a distant fantasy, he plows his fingers into me drilling hard.

He milks the dripping honey from my channel while his mouth sucks one rocket blast of orgasm after another from my already quivering flesh.

I scream again and again. I can't survive all the climaxes he's giving me, but I have to survive it. I can't stop him—not when this feels so incredibly good.

He drives deep into my tissues mauling me in low, guttural snarls of hungry satisfaction.

His strong hands control my movements at the same time that he keeps kneading, gripping, and compressing my thighs and ass.

I thrash against the wall in torrential ecstasy. I practically dissolve in a puddle of goo when he finally stands up.

My slit quivers and spasms when he drags his fingers out of me. He delivers one last lick to my enflamed tissues and he still has to hold me steady when he straightens up to face me.

I sob and whimper in front of him. I can't look at him. I'm still ragged from all of this.

He doesn't give me a chance even to get my head together before he scoops me up in his arms and carries me into the other room.

I hold onto him for dear life. He's taking me into his bedroom.

He drops on his knees on the bed, lays me down on the bed with my pants still around my thighs, and sinks down on the mattress next to me kissing me.

His warm breath floats into my nostrils. His hands caress me all over and graze the sensitive bare skin of my hip.

I shudder at that touch. It blasts me into another whirlwind of sensation. I don't have to wonder where this is going.

He feels me shudder, breaks away from kissing me, and pushes himself up on his elbow.

He keeps looking up into my eyes with that deep, penetrating, smoking hot stare of his. We both know we want this.

He looks down at my naked lower body—except that I'm still wearing my brace. He couldn't pull my pants down any farther without taking the brace off.

He grabs the leather strap around my thigh and tugs it loose. The feeling rushes straight to my crotch and I gasp out as the heat floods me.

John used to do this. He used to take my brace off when he undressed me.

Duke looks up at me and sees me panting and flushing with deep, insatiable desire. He's touching and handling my body like I'm already his. He already knows I want him. I'll do anything to get him.

I gulp as the truth sinks in. What is he going to do once he takes my brace off?

My mind swims from so many pictures, fantasies, possibilities, and desires.

"Duke?" I choke.

He glances up at me. "Hmmm?"

"I'm....I'm not on any birth control."

His head shoots up and he freezes staring at me.

I wince under that stare. "I...I should have told you....at the beach...." I falter. "I went off of it after John died. I thought....." I clamp my eyes shut. "I guess I wanted to shoot the finger at the univ erse....because I thought I would never do it with anyone again—or at least not so soon—not like this."

He doesn't move for a second. His hand remains frozen on my thigh. He doesn't take my brace the rest of the way off.

I cringe when I see myself lying half-naked in front of him. I should leave right now. I should run for it and we can forget this ever happened.

What is he going to say? How will he respond—by saying he'll use a condom? I'm sure he doesn't have one so soon after Naomi's death.

I shut my eyes and look away. I'll have to re-tighten my brace before I stand up.

Then I can get the hell out of here as soon as humanly possible.

At least Duke and I won't see each other at work—except when he comes to the hospital after calls.

I can deal with that. I can deal with seeing him at firehouse barbecues. We'll just go back to being firehouse acquaintances—the way we're supposed to be.

I'm just thinking about how I can make the most tactful possible exit when he suddenly comes back to life.

His expression softens and he raises one hand to cradle my cheek. He doesn't let me look away.

"We could do this," he murmurs. "We could do it anyway."

"But....I might get pregnant. What about.....?" My mind turns another somersault.

What about Amelia....and his baby.....and....and everything?

Is he really saying he would want to get me pregnant....so soon after losing his whole family?

Chapter 17: Ellen

Duke looks away first after just dropping the bomb on me that he would do it with me to get me pregnant. "We don't have to if you don't want to....." he mumbles.

"Wait a minute!" I dive for him to hold him back. "Are you serious?! I mean....serious?! You really want to....."

"Why not?" he asks.

"But you....." I can't even say it. I can't believe we're actually having this conversation.

"What were you and John doing about it?" he asks like we're talking about buying a new toaster or something.

I blink at him in stupid shock. Is this man really asking me about... *.that?*

He waits for me to answer. He blinks at me like I'm making a big deal about nothing.

"You would...you would really want to......" I can't even say the words.

"Why not?" he asks again. "I always wanted kids—though the universe seems to have other plans for me. You know what? Forget I said anything." He starts to sit up. "Never mind."

"Hey!" I bellow and shoot off the bed. I grab him a lot harder than I should. "Stop right there! Why are you saying, 'why not' one minute and then telling me to forget about it the next? What the hell is going on here?!"

He looks away and his features pinched. "You don't know. No one knows. I only told Naomi."

"Told her what?"

Now he's the one who gulps. He won't look at me. "Everyone I try to have kids with....they leave...or they die. I wouldn't want that to happen to you."

I realize from a great distance that I'm holding onto his arm in a death grip. "What are you talking about?!" I gasp. "Why would it happen to me?"

"My first wife....before Naomi.....she got pregnant....." His voice chokes. He keeps his head turned away so I can't see him. He has to fight to get the words out. "She developed some kind of psychosis where she thought the baby was eating her alive from the inside. She aborted the child and vanished out of my life." He looks down at the bedspread and mumbles in a dull undertone. "Naomi and I.....we were going to change all that. That's the whole reason we got together....so we could do it together.....and now that's gone."

I stare at the side of his face. "Is that why you want to get with me?"

"NO!!" He spins around fast. "NO!! You can't think that! That isn't why I said it—not at all! I wasn't trying to say that. Don't think that. I swear that isn't the reason."

"Okay," I murmur. "I believe you."

"I just thought....I don't know what I thought. I thought maybe you and John...." He shakes that thought away. "Just forget it. I didn't mean to offend you." He starts to move away like he's the one who wants to get the hell out of here.

"You didn't offend me, Duke," I insist. "I just.....I never really thought about it before."

His head shoots up again. "You never thought about it?! Like—not ever?! Weren't you and John planning to have kids of your own?"

"We...." I stare into space trying to get my brain back into gear.

Duke waits for me to say something. I have to pull my head out of the clouds to think clearly about this.

"I......I honestly can't remember now if John and I ever talked about having kids of our own." I cover my eyes and groan. "I can't believe we're actually talking about this."

"Well, if you aren't on birth control and we're even thinking about doing it with each other, then we have to talk about it, don't we? Either that or we have to wait until you are on birth control if you really don't want to have kids of your own."

"It isn't that. I was on birth control when I met him. Then I just stayed on it the whole time we were together. We never talked about it. Things were already so complicated with him taking care of Oakleigh and fitting our schedules together and everything. It never came up....and then....after he died.....one of the first things I did was to throw away my pills. I did it in protest of the whole situation—to show the universe how mad I was that it took him away from me."

He doesn't laugh. He doesn't turn it into a joke or anything like that.

He gazes back at me listening to me talk about something I never even talked to my own husband about.

"Do you want kids?" Duke finally asks. "I mean, would you want them if he was still alive or if you never met him."

"Yes! I mean....I never really let myself think about when I would have them....."

I cringe again when I realize I'm having this conversation with a man I just came perilously close to having sex with. I almost just lost my widow's virginity to this man.

I flinch at those words, but what the hell? What do I really have to lose here?

"I understand if you don't want to do it with me," he begins. "I'm no prize...."

"Hey!" I counter. "Stop that. Are you seriously saying you would want to go there with me? We're....we aren't even dating! We just kissed for the first time less than an hour ago."

He shrugs. "Naomi and I weren't dating when we got together, either. We hadn't even kissed when we decided to get together and start a family together."

I gape at him in shock. "Are you serious?"

He nods. "She quit the Fire Service because she decided she wanted kids. We knew we were attracted to each other, but we couldn't act on it as long as she worked for me. I asked her to stay in town and go out with me. She said yes. We both knew it meant starting a family."

"So.....that was before....."

"Before the barbecue. We talked about it on the beach....and then we did it for the first time. Things went downhill from there when we got Amelia.....and then we found out Naomi was pregnant. That's the whole story."

I blink at him in stupid disbelief. "And you actually would want to do it that way again?"

He makes a face. "If you can get past the idea that I'm bad luck and that I have some kind of cursed albatross hanging around my neck that causes pregnant women to either get killed or go insane, then yes, I would jump at the chance to do it again. I only suggested it because I thought you and John might have been talking about it or planning it or maybe even trying. I thought maybe you would want to go ahead and do it now—like maybe you didn't want to wait any longer—kind of like I don't want to wait any longer."

"But.....but what if things didn't work out between us?" I stammer. "What if we decide we really hate each other? Then we would get stuck co-parenting a child when we can't stand the sight of each other."

He actually bursts out laughing. "I think I know you well enough to say that wouldn't happen. We like and respect each other. We both know the other would do right by the child—or children. We would work together even if we decided not to be a couple with each other. I know you're a caring mother. I've seen the way you act around Oakleigh and she isn't even yours."

I look away and tears spring to my eyes when I remember Amelia. God, he loved her so much!

No one in the world would ever have known she was adopted. Ellis didn't know when he lost his memory. He thought Amelia was Duke's naturally born baby.

I choke on the words. "I know you're a good father, too."

Out of nowhere, he slips his hand into mine. "I think you're the greatest thing ever," he half-whispers. "I think you're sweet, kind, caring, professional, and unbelievably hot. I really envy John for being married to you. If you want to do that with me, I'm your man. I'm right here whenever you want me. You only have to say the word."

I look up at him and open my mouth to answer, but the words won't come.

He sees me struggling, and without hesitation, he scoots up the bed, folds me in his arms, and lies back on the bed to hold me.

He pulls my head down on his chest. "It's all right," he whispers into my hair. "No one is going to pressure you into doing anything."

I finally allow myself to voice my worst fears. "What if I screw it up with my own child the way I screwed up with Oakleigh?" I clamp my eyes shut to hold back tears. "What if someone decides my own child is better off with someone else?"

"Then you just have to decide to love the child as much as you can for as long as it lasts," he murmurs back. "That's what we had to do with Amelia. We didn't know if her mother would come along and take Amelia away from us. We just had to make up our minds to give her the best home and the best set of parents we could. We had to shower her with as much love as possible so she would understand that she had two parents who loved her. That's the best we could do."

I clamp my eyes shut against those words. The obvious love in his voice stabs me in the heart.

He would feel that way about any child he and I had together. He would hazard any danger and risk absolutely anything for his child.

I already know what kind of husband and father he would be. I've seen him with Naomi and Amelia all this time.

I could have that kind of happiness.

I only have to remember Naomi carrying Amelia around at firehouse barbecues and weddings to remember how happy she was. There never was a baby more showered in love than Amelia.

I don't blame Duke for wanting to get that back.

So what about me? Is that what I want?

It would be so easy for me to say that raising Oakleigh is too complicated already—except that it isn't.

Raising one child isn't that complicated—not even raising her alone. I'm lucky because I have the Brewers helping me out.

Now Oakleigh will be spending equal time with me, Keith's family, and Danny's family. I'll only have her one week out of three.

Plenty of women raise more children than that with a lot less. So what's stopping me?

I summon all my courage to say it, but I still can't speak above a whisper. "I want to do it."

He doesn't even flinch. "Are you sure you want to do it with me?"

I have to shut my eyes before I whisper, "Yes."

"Then take me," he murmurs. "I'm not going to force it on you. If you want me, come and get me. I'm all yours."

Chapter 18: Ellen

I take a minute to decide what I'm going to do and how. I don't want to jump on top of Duke and ravish him like a fresh-faced milkmaid. That would be ridiculous.

I pry myself out of his arms, swivel over to the edge of the bed, and stand up next to it. He lies there watching me. Does he think I'm going to get dressed and leave?

I can't stop myself from blushing when I start unbuttoning my shirt. His eyes widen and then he swivels off the bed, too.

He sits on the edge of the mattress in front of me. His eyes glow with so much light when he stares up at me from below.

I pull my shirt off and then slither out of my bra. His warm hands caress up and down my hips while he watches me in appreciative awe. He knows what I'm doing.

I drop my clothes on the floor. He's seeing me naked. He knows I want this.

I'm about to do it with him. I could get pregnant with his child.

The thought intoxicates me out of my mind. I want that. I want it with him. I definitely want it with him and no one else.

I take hold of my brace strap, unbuckle it, and shift my weight to my good leg to hold myself up while I take my brace and pants off.

I start to bend over to unbuckle the ankle strap, but Duke does it for me.

He pulls the brace away and he doesn't sit back up.

He kisses up my bare hip to my stomach and leaves a blistering trail of hot, moist, mouth bites across my sensitive mound.

My flesh trembles for him. I want all of him. I want his mouth on my swollen tissues. I want his fingers inside me. I want his body pulsating his seed deep into my core.

He eases my pants down my thighs. I quiver when the fabric grazes my sensitive flesh.

He pushes my pants and my panties down to the bottom of my bad leg. I can't bend my knee to take them off, so he does it for me.

I steady myself by resting my hands on his shoulders. He feels strong, protective, and enticing like this. I want to disintegrate into his heat.

He straightens up. I can't take my weight off my good leg to step out of my pants, but that doesn't matter.

His eyes burn into me from below. He wants this so bad. He wants everything we could be and become together.

I see it all in his eyes and I want that, too. I never realized before how much I do want it.

He eases me closer toward him and scoops his arms around my naked body. He's still fully dressed. That's for me to take care of. He said he wouldn't do it for me.

As soon as I feel him pulling me forward, I know what I have to do. I push his shoulders backward to lie him down on the mattress.

He responds by climbing up to the pillows and stretching out there. His eyes devour me with so much hungry madness. His body strains under his clothes. God, he's magnificent!

I crawl onto the bed on my hands and one knee. My bad leg drags, but I really don't care.

I didn't spend all this time being married to John without learning how to use this leg to my advantage.

I crawl up his body ever so slowly. I feel how smoky hot I'm looking at him. I'm about to do it with him. I'm about to take his naked seed into my body.

Some forgotten instinct tells me that I will get pregnant from this. If I don't get pregnant today, we'll probably keep doing it until it happens.

I hitch my bad leg up so I can crawl all the way up to his mouth and pour out all my fervent passion into that kiss. I ache for him. My body throbs and trembles from hunger for him.

His hands come to rest on my naked body. He glides up my sides, fondles my breasts until I moan, and then his fingers plunge between my legs to finger my saturated lips.

I groan as the energy rises, but that isn't what we agreed.

I push his hand away and wind up pinning his wrists to the mattress on either side of his shoulders.

I smirk at him when I see what I'm doing, but I let him go immediately.

A flash of pure exhilarated excitement crosses his face when I look at him like that. I'm going to do this. To hell with it. I want him. Now I'm going to get him.

I straddle his hips and ride down on his bulging package just to get the message across.

He lets out a little gasp through his nose and his stomach contracts when I stroke against his crotch.

I grab his shirt and pull it up. He's just as chiseled and solid underneath as I knew he would be.

He flexes upright just enough for me to pull his shirt off. Then he relaxes back on the bed.

He doesn't touch me until I start kissing him again. I kiss him much more deeply and drag my bare breasts, my whole naked body, and my dripping slit all over him.

His hardness feels amazing between my legs—and then his hands take over.

He scoops one hand up to the back of my neck. He flattens the other against the small of my back and arches me down into his hips.

He digs his swollen bulge into my sensitive tissues enough to make me squeal, and before I know it, I can't stop grinding on him in another punishing orgasm.

I buck and scream into his mouth again. His pants get in the way. I can't get to him when our bodies press against each other like this.

He grips my breasts in one hand, wraps one arm around my waist, and brings me down harder on his spike.

I collapse on top of him moaning and trembling, but this isn't what we agreed on, either. I want to go all the way.

I push myself up to look down at him. I have to blink the stars out of my eyes so I can focus on him.

I can't smile anymore. I realize I'm glaring at him, but this insatiable ravenous lust won't stop now.

My lips pout open. I tremble on the crest of something huge—something that will change my life forever. That's what this is. That's what he is. He's the storm that will destroy the wreckage of my old life and make a new one grow.

My hands land on his iron chest and follow the furrow of his abs down to his waistband. He lies back on the bed watching me in so much haunting profound emotion.

I can't even tell what that emotion is. It looks like awe.

His body tenses when I touch him, but his hands won't stop ranging all over me. He touches, strokes, and grips my arms down to my wrists to guide my hands to his waist.

He squeezes my breasts, grips my hips, and rocks me on a slow, never-ending wave of bliss to drive himself between my legs.

I unbutton his pants. His zipper strains when I pass it across his throbbing shaft.

I move over onto my good leg to pull his pants off, but he does that for me, too.

He pushes his pants, socks, shorts, and shoes onto the floor. They land with a thump at the foot of the bed.

He lies back and stretches out where he was before. His tool sticks straight up at me. He's ready for me.

I throw my good leg over him again and straddle him with both of us naked now, but I still don't want to just jump him and be done with it. That feels too crass and sudden even though we've been working toward this for so long.

I know that now. We've been working toward this for a long time—long before Naomi died—maybe even since before Duke and Naomi even got together.

I was with her when she welcomed him to that first barbecue. I was with him in the hospital. This has been coming for a long time.

Maybe the simple fact that he became Fire Chief in John's place ordained that he and I would end up together.

I lean over and kiss him. We both fall into each other's warm so much more fervently now. We both know this only ends one way.

I arch into him and stroke my juicy flesh down his rigid shaft. He groans in ecstasy when I start stroking faster.

His hard length feels majestic against my clit. I can't get enough of it. My juices coat his ridges. A thrill rushes through me and then starts to spread outward to the rest of my body.

I feel myself starting to spiral into another climax just from the stimulation against my clitoris. My eyes roll back in my head and I groan into his mouth.

He pushes me back just enough so he can see my eyes. I'm skyrocketing out of control too fast.

Before I realize what's happening, he grabs me around the waist again in a tight embrace of both arms locked together.

He pushes his hips up, and unbelievably fast, he thrusts quick and hard to stroke his shaft against my clit. He doesn't penetrate. He just teases me until I succumb to a mind-blowing orgasm.

I want to huddle in his arms, but he won't let me. He kisses me, but he never releases my eyes. He holds my gaze so he can see me fall apart on his granite shaft.

He eases off as I power down....until the moment when he glides inside.

I freeze staring into the bottomless depths of his eyes. Everything we've been doing—everything I've been doing—prepares me for this moment.

His thickness expands my already clenched channel and floods my senses with heat and exhilarating energy.

I can't move. I stay locked above him feeling every blistering inch of him drilling into my core. I can't stop these waves of pleasure sweeping out to take me over.

They wipe all resistance. This is what it means—us being together. This is the moment when it happens—this moment of highest connection and togetherness between us.

Past and present become one. There is no separation. I could actually believe John and Naomi are here in the room with us—loving us, approving of us, encouraging us.

Amelia, Duke's unborn baby, and all the children that ever could be between me and Duke—they're all in this room. They're all coming together.

Time doesn't exist here. It's pure love with nothing in between.

I can't even see Duke anymore. His eyes show me windows into galaxies and centuries—millennia spread out in a web of interconnected families existing throughout time.

The power shooting from his shaft into my being won't let me float out there, though. His thrusts draw me back to reality—back to him.

He flexes his abs to drive his hips up into me. He gives a little corkscrew motion at the top of each stroke to drill it in extra deep.

His nostrils flare and a sudden burst of white-hot lightning shoots into me every time he does it. His essence spreads through me in delicious, delirious waves.

He breaks off my mouth and pushes me up. "Sit up, baby," he whispers. "I want to see you."

I sit back on his hips. His spike lies buried deeper than deep in my innermost being.

My vision keeps slipping out of focus when I rock on him. Mind-blowing explosions keep flashing before my eyes.

I brace my hands on his chest to steady myself as I spiral out of this world, but I keep floating back to the awareness of him lying beneath me.

He gazes up at me with that deep awed expression of rapturous passion. His hands possess my breasts, my face, my waist, my hips, my thighs.

He pulls me into his beat. Each collision shoots another catastrophic wave of orgasmic pleasure to my deepest core. Is this the signal for my body to ovulate? Can my body hear his body speaking to me—calling on me to give him children?

Thinking that erupts my soul to smithereens. I throw back my head and moan out all the rising torrential passion about to break me open.

As soon as I fall back, he seizes me in an unbreakable grip. "Come on!" he calls out. "Come on! Do it now!"

I can't stop myself from doing it. I throw myself down on his tool so impossibly hard, but he's already bucking up into me from below.

He steers my hips down onto his thrusts to shatter me into a million pieces. His body commands me to respond and I start to scream as the climactic release breaks over me.

I can't do it anymore. I can't move myself hard enough or fast enough. I'm flying out of control, but he doesn't stop.

He slams into me and pulls me down at the same time. Our rhythm synchronizes. He bumps me up hard enough to make my breasts bounce to his rhythm….and then the hot jet of his essence invades me with unstoppable heat.

I peak again when I feel our bodies join. His load spreads through me and takes over all the cells of my body.

I fall forward to sink onto his chest, but he's already lunging off the bed, scooping me onto his lap, and flipping me onto my back.

He arches between my legs again and again to pump me full of himself. I float in a daydream of endless bliss feeling his seed take hold of me and bring me back to life.

Chapter 19: Duke

I rummage in the supply closet of the firehouse training room and pull out a bunch of nasopharyngeal airways, endotracheal airways, and mannequins. I lay everything out on the tables to get ready for this morning's training session.

Just then, Caleb sticks his head through the door. "Duke!"

"What?" I yell over my shoulder.

"The replacement truck is here! The driver is parking it outside. He wants to drive back in ours. Should we unload all the gear?"

"Yes!" I tell him. "Tell the driver to go up to the breakroom and wait there 'cuz this is gonna take a while. Do a full truck inspection on the new vehicle and then transfer everything to the new truck."

"What do you mean by everything?" he asks. "What about the hoses?"

"Everything," I repeat. "Anything that isn't actually attached to the truck body and anything you might want to use on any call, no matter how obscure. Empty the truck of everything—absolutely everything." He turns to leave. "And then come back and get me before he leaves so I can check it!"

He waves behind him and disappears. I go back to what I'm doing, but I have to work hard to stop myself from letting my mind drift back to Ellen.

She spent all of last night with me in my apartment—in my bed.

Holy crap, that woman knows how to make love! I've never met anyone like her. She's teaching me things not even Naomi knew.

I have to concentrate on work and not think about everything we did and everything I still want to do with her.

She drove me to work this morning and we kissed in the parking lot before she went to work at the hospital. Jesus, she makes my nuts hurt just from thinking about her!

I never want her to go home. I know she has to. I just dread the day when Keith and Danny find out she isn't spending any of her time away from Oakleigh at the old house—the house Ellen shared with John.

I could have gotten her pregnant last night. The idea gives me an unbelievable thrill.

I don't ever wonder if Naomi would approve. She worshiped Ellen. Everyone does.

I have to think. I have to pay attention. I set up the mannequins and all the airways and everything else I need for the training session.

The noise out in the garage gets louder. I should probably go out there and check on the transfer of equipment—not to mention the new truck itself.

There might be something wrong with it. Then we would have to send the new truck back and keep the old one. That would be a massive waste of time.

I'm just about to leave when Caleb comes back. "We transferred everything, Duke—and we ran the truck inspection on the new vehicle."

"I better come take a look at this inspection."

He leads the way out to the garage, but right then, the firehouse alarm goes off.

Everyone in the garage freezes, including me. We all look up at the ceiling and then at each other.

"What do we do?" Brooke asks.

"Take the new truck," I tell them. "Go! Run the call the way you normally would! Go!"

They all take off running for the new truck. It's still parked out on the driveway pad in front of our usual rescue truck.

Keith has to reverse out of the driveway onto the street before they can leave. Then the ladder truck and the two ambulances follow.

I'm the last one left in the firehouse—apart from the maintenance driver, of course.

He comes downstairs just as I'm about to walk out to my support pickup. "Great!" he exclaims. "I'll be on my way now. See you later."

"No, you won't. The crew just got a call. You have to stay until the truck comes back. Then I'll inspect it and then we'll do the handover—not before."

His jaw drops. "But that could take hours!"

"Yep. You can make yourself comfortable in the breakroom or you can stay somewhere else. It's up to you. Just give me your phone number and I'll call or text you when we're ready to sign off on the truck."

"But the crew could be out all night!" he protests. "They could get back-to-back calls and I could be stuck here until tomorrow morning!"

I nod. "That is a distinct possibility, yes."

"What am I supposed to do—get a hotel room? I don't have an executive expense account, you know."

"You can stay upstairs in the crew bunk room if you want to. You'll have it all to yourself if the crew is out working." I walk away. "I gotta go. Don't touch that truck or it will be your job."

I don't have any more time to waste on this. I head to my support pickup, slam the door, and turn the dashboard computer to the dispatch notes.

The crew is heading for another car accident on the highway, but right then, another alert code comes through the computer.

The call is a gas leak/possible explosion at the elementary school.

I snatch the radio and hit the throttle in a rush.

Keith answers the radio. "Rescue 1, en route to...."

"Send Ladder 1 and EMS Unit 1 back to the elementary school Priority 1!" I order. "We just got another call! I repeat! Send Ladder 1 and EMS Unit 1 to Howe Elementary School Priority 1! Rescue 1 and EMS Unit 2 will have to handle the car accident on their own."

Keith changes his tone in a flash. "You got it! Ladder 1 and EMS Unit 1 diverting now!"

I hang up and hit the gas burning rubber out of the parking lot. It will take the ladder truck and ambulance at least twenty minutes to get all the way back here from the highway.

I'm the only person within response distance. I have to get to the school now.

I skid to a halt in front of the office and storm onto the grounds. The principal meets me at the gate and opens his mouth to tell me what's going on.

All the color drains from his face. "Where's the rest of the crew? Where are the trucks and ambulances?"

"They're on their way from another call. I'm it for now."

His eyes fall out of their sockets. "Just you?!"

I stride past him. "What do you got? What's the situation?"

He races after me talking fast. "There was an explosion in the junior wing....and then we smelled gas. We don't know where it came from.

We don't even know where the explosion came from. We tried to evacuate...."

The scene in front of me answers the rest of my questions. The students and staff completely abandon their usual orderly evacuation plan.

They abandon the school just as fast. People run shoving and yelling from every classroom in no order at all.

At least they have the presence of mind to all rush in the same direction—toward the basketball courts which is their usual disaster assembly point.

It takes a long, long time for the teachers to organize all the kids by class. This makes it astronomically more difficult for the teachers to take a head count to find out if anyone is missing.

"We contacted the city about turning off the gas to the building," the principal tells me. "I don't know if they did it yet."

"Call them back and tell them it's an emergency and we need it shut off right now."

"Hey! Where are you going?!" he asks.

"I'm going to check the building. You stay here and make sure to keep everyone contained on the basketball courts. Don't let anyone near the building."

I take off by myself and make a tour of the school to see if anything is out of place. It is.

I get all the way around the other side of the building. I don't see anything out of the ordinary until I pass the gym.

I'm just about to call it quits and go back to the basketball courts when I spot one of the classrooms at the very far end of the building. This explains why no one else saw what or where the problem was.

Flames billow against the windows from inside. The fire doesn't seem to have spread anywhere else. It's all trapped inside that one classroom.

I rush over there, but I would have to go through the entire school building to get to that classroom the normal way.

I rush to the emergency exit at the far end of the building. This one door leads into the burning classroom. This emergency exit is the quickest way inside.

I move my hand closer to the door latch, but the heat radiating through the door stops me from touching it.

I step back, kick the door open, and an almighty boom of flames rockets through the opening from inside. Noise and heat thump the air.

I duck away and squint into the flames. I can't see anything in there.

I should have put on my turnouts before I came over here, but it's too late to change that now.

Chapter 20: Duke

I wait for the draft to die down, but the fire in the classroom doesn't diminish.

I wouldn't normally go into a burning building without my turnouts and an SCBA, but right at that moment, I spot a young female teacher and a cluster of students hiding under a table across the room.

They've taken refuge against a wall. They're protected from the fire for now, but they won't stay that way.

I glance around for anything I can use to protect myself. I don't see anything until I notice a wooden bookshelf a few feet inside the door.

The bookshelf isn't on fire yet and it looks light enough for me to carry. I grab it, shake the books off it, and raise it in my arms to use as a shield.

I position the shelf between myself and the worst of the flames. From what I can tell, they're coming from one wall of the room—and I definitely smell gas.

The flames crawl across the ceiling and head for the open emergency exit door, now that fresh air is flowing into the room. That leaves a little bit of space near the floor.

I duck as low as I can, but I have to stay upright so I can move fast. The heat burns my arms and face, but I have to get these kids out.

I charge in and dive down on my knees on the floor by their table. I use the bookshelf to block the heat from getting to any of us.

"Stay behind me!" I yell over the noise. "The Fire Department is on the way! Follow me and I'll get you out!" I look up at the teacher. "Is this everyone?"

She yells something back, but I can't hear her over the noise. She says something about, ".....bathroom....." and waves toward the other side of the room—the side connected to the rest of the school building.

I don't have time to ask for clarification. "Follow me! Stay behind me!"

I stand up and grit my teeth when another jet of flames scorches me all over.

The teacher grabs the kids and pulls them out from under the table. They cower behind me while I hold the bookshelf between us and the flames.

I have to move slower on my way to the door. The kids cringe and whimper as the heat becomes more punishing, but I have to keep going.

I stand by the door holding the shelf raised while the teacher pushes the kids outside. "Get to the basketball court!" I tell her. "Take everyone away from the building!"

She turns around to say something to me, but I can't wait. The fire will only get worse.

I charge back inside, and this time, I don't slow down.

I sprint my fastest to the other side of the room, blast through the other door leading into the school, and slam the door behind me.

I let the bookshelf fall out of my exhausted arms. The fire is still contained inside that one classroom. It doesn't penetrate this far—not yet.

I gasp for breath, but the heat coming through the wall makes up my mind for me. If anyone is trapped in here, I have to get them out right away.

I have to hunt around before I even find the bathrooms. The smell of gas stings my nostrils here, too. If the fire gets out of that classroom, it will cause a massive explosion and take out the whole school.

I don't have much time. I stick my head into the boys' bathroom. "Is anyone in here?!" I yell. "I'm with the Fire Department!"

Nothing. I move on. The next bathroom is the staff bathroom. It's also empty.

I finally make it to the girls' bathroom. If I don't find anyone in here, I'm going to have to pull out for my own safety. I can't let myself get trapped in this building, either—not with all this gas around.

I barge into the girls' bathroom and start pushing open the stall doors. "Is anyone in here?!" I bellow. "I'm with the Fire Department! I'm here to get you out of the building!"

"Help me!" a little girl whimpers from one of the farthest stalls.

I storm over there, push open the stall, and see Oakleigh Brewer sitting on the floor next to the toilet.

She sits with her legs sticking out in front of her—and one of her legs bends at the wrong angle below the knee.

She whimpers in terror when she sees me. Her lower lip trembles and her eyes dart around at the stall walls.

"Help me!" she whimpers again.

I find myself smiling at her as I step into the stall and kneel down in front of her. "Hey, sweetie!" I murmur. "Don't worry! I'm gonna get you out."

She glances down at her leg and immediately looks away. "There was an earthquake!" she stammers. "I fell over....and....I can't stand u p....."

"Okay, sweetie," I breathe. "Nothing to worry about. I'll get you out, but we have to hurry."

I glance around again thinking fast.

"What's wrong?" she asks.

I hesitate before I tell her the truth. "Listen to me, sweetheart. There's a fire in the school. That's why I'm here. Everyone is out of the building except for you. Do you smell that rotten smell? That's the smell of escaping gas."

She nods down at her broken leg. "My dad told me."

"That's really good, but the smell means the fire will come here soon, too. We need to get out now. Normally, I would splint your leg, but I have to carry you out like this. It will probably hurt a lot, but we'll make it work. Okay? We can't stay in here any longer. It isn't safe."

She nods. "Okay." She starts crying for real this time. "Just get me out of here!"

"Oh, baby," I murmur. "Come on. We gotta go."

I can't wait for her to try to stand up on her good leg. I scoop her up in my arms.

She screams in pain, but I can't wait around for the other shoe to drop.

I carry her screaming and crying out of the bathroom, kick the door open, and get out into the main school corridor. I don't dare go back toward the burning classroom.

I head for the main building entrance near the office. I just want to put as much distance as possible between myself and the fire.

Oakleigh huddles in my arms. I try not to bump her leg around too much. If the gas smell isn't so bad near the lobby, I could stop to splint her leg there.

Getting her out of the building and removing her to a safe distance is more important right now.

I make it halfway to the lobby when the radio crackles on my shoulder. "Duke!" Theo Gough calls. "Where are you?"

I can't take my hands off Oakleigh to answer him, but I hear the ladder truck siren in the distance. Thank God the crew is here. The paramedics will take care of Oakleigh for me.

I pick up the pace, but at that moment, a bone-crushing thump goes off behind me.

The explosion envelops the building behind me and invades the corridor.

The concussion knocks me over and I pitch flat on my face. I do my best to fall on top of Oakleigh to shield her with my body.

She screams again when we hit the floor. Blistering pain scorches me through the back of my T-shirt and I bellow in agony as my skin blisters. How much longer do I have?

The draft pulls back toward the first classroom and then another monstrous wave of flames covers the ceiling.

The heat turns the corridor into a death trap except for a few feet of space right against the floor. I don't dare to stand up this time.

The skin on my back screams in pain—and that's nothing compared to Oakleigh's screams. I can't tell if she's screaming in pain or fear. It's probably both.

I glance around in desperation. I have to get to the lobby, but it's too far away. I would have to drag Oakleigh across the floor to get there. That would take too long.

I will have to drag her anywhere I take her. Whatever way I use to get her out of the building, I have to do it quickly.

I almost collapse in relief when I notice the staffroom nearby. It's right next to us. The door stands open and I look out through the windows.

The basketball court is right there....and the fire crew swarms the school grounds rolling out their hoses. I'm only a few feet away from help and safety.

"Hold on, sweetie!" I yell to Oakleigh. "Hold on! We aren't done yet!"

She's crying too hard to answer me. I know what I have to do.

I push myself up a few inches. I don't dare even to get up on my hands and knees.

I drag myself toward the staffroom, take hold of Oakleigh's shirt collar behind her neck, and pull.

I slide her one painstaking inch at a time across the floor and into the staffroom. I kick the door shut behind me.

The door and walls protect us from the fire, but that won't last long, either. I glance up at the window.

It's high enough that I'll have to lift Oakleigh out of it. I'll probably have to hold her while I climb through it. None of the crew knows where I am. They won't be able to help me until I get out of the building on my own.

I turn back to Oakleigh. She sobs and wails in terror while she hauls herself to the nearest wall and props herself in a sitting position.

"We're almost out, sweetie!" I pant. "I'm gonna splint your leg and then break this window."

She's too hysterical even to hear me. She keeps bursting into sobs and looking everywhere but at me.

I stagger to my feet, grab the nearest table, and swing it over my head to break the legs off. These will be perfect for splinting her knee.

I lay two broken table legs on either side of her knee. My T-shirt hangs in rags off my shoulders, so I rip it off, tear it into strips, and start binding the splint together.

I don't try to correct the alignment of the break. I just check the pulse at her ankle to make sure she still has one. The rest will have to wait until we get outside.

She screams when I tighten the bindings. I glance up at her once and find her staring at me.

"Duke....." Her features spasm all over the place. She has a hard time controlling her mouth.

"Yeah, sweetie?!" I pant.

"I'm sorry.....about....Ellen....and everything...."

I burst out in a grin of pure relief. "That's okay, sweetie." I dive in and give her a kiss on the forehead just out of impulse. "I know you've been really upset about losing your dad. Don't worry about it."

"You lost your baby......" Her voice breaks. "And now Naomi is dead...." She breaks down sobbing hard.

I find it easy to forget that Oakleigh was close to Naomi before I ever met any of these people. Naomi was part of Oakleigh's firehouse family for years.

I grab the girl, hug her against my chest, and kiss her hair. Her body racks with sobs.

The sound of her broken voice brings tears to my eyes. This poor kid has been through the meat grinder—much worse than I have.

I wish I could comfort her as long as she needs me to, but we can already hear flames thumping and whoofing outside this room.

I push her back, hold onto her shoulders, and get into her face. "We gotta get out of here, baby. We don't have any time left to worry about that. I'm gonna break that window and then carry you outside. When I pick you up, I need you to hold onto me super tight around my neck. Understand? You hold on as tight as you can. Don't worry about hurting me. Understand?"

She nods fast, but she's still sobbing her eyes out. I can't wait.

I stand up, pick up a nearby chair, and smash it through the window. At the same moment, another blast of flames blows the staffroom door open.

Oakleigh screams as fire plumes into the room. I snatch her off the floor as gently as I can, but I can only hold onto her with one arm. I need to use the other to climb out the window.

"Hold onto me!" I yell in her ear. "Don't let go!"

She straps her little arms around my neck in a crushing grip. Good. I want her here right against me.

I lunge for the broken window and cut my hands and arms on the glass shards, but I don't care. I jump out of the window onto the pavement just as fire consumes the staffroom.

Firefighters and paramedics surround us. Sophie and Allison try to take Oakleigh away from me, but she won't let go.

I walk straight past the crew to the waiting ambulance. I don't see any other patients. We're the only ones who need medical attention.

I climb into the back and try to put Oakleigh on the gurney. Sophie and Allison move in to take Oakleigh's vital signs.

"We're safe, baby," I gasp. "We're safe. Lie down here so the paramedics can take a look at you...."

She won't let go. She keeps wailing in my ear. "Don't leave me, Duke! Don't leave me!"

"I'm not going anywhere, baby. I'm right here." I have to physically pry her arms off me so I can put her down. "I'm here. I'm not going anywhere. I'm here."

As soon as I get her off me, she grabs my hand and won't let go. I hesitate to break that grip.

I glance outside and see the fire crew surrounding the building—or the crew is surrounding the building as well as they can with so few people.

I should go out there and help them, but right then, Sophie's voice drifts into my ear from inches away. "Sit down, Duke."

I look up. "Huh? What's wrong?"

She gives me one of those looks. "I said sit down. You aren't going anywhere but to the hospital."

I don't know what she means, but almost at the same time, Allison presses a large gauze pad to my shoulder.

Blood saturates the pad instantly. I have a massive gash on my shoulder. I didn't even feel it until right now.

I look down at myself and see my whole chest covered in blood from cuts from the broken glass.

That moment switches back on the pain sensors in my back. I'm covered in burns and deep slashes.

I sink onto the bench next to the gurney. Sophie is right. I'm one of the patients.

Sophie takes Oakleigh's vital signs, but the girl is fine. She just has a broken leg.

The two paramedics spend a lot more time working on me. They bandage up all my cuts to stop the bleeding. Then they put a big air-occlusion dressing on my back to cover the burn.

Oakleigh doesn't let go of my hand even once, not even after the paramedics finish with her.

She sinks back on the pillow sniffling and grimacing, but I can see now that it's mostly just from nerves and the leftover fear from the call. She knows where she is and she isn't in any more danger.

I don't have the heart to let go of her hand, either—not after all the problems we've been having with each other—or all the problems she's been having with me.

I'm too grateful to put it behind us.

Chapter 21: Ellen

I slot my latest chart into the stack of files at the nurses' station and take out another one. I still have five more patients to triage from the car accident on the highway.

They're all walking wounded. All the critical cases are upstairs in surgery by now.

I'm just turning around to go check on my next patient when Keith comes up to me.

"Hey, sweetheart," I greet him. "Are you guys all done with the car accident scene?"

He doesn't smile. He scowls at me in his serious way. "There was another call, darlin'. There was a gas leak and an explosion at the school. Oakleigh is on her way over in the other ambulance."

My heart stops. "What happened to her?! How critical is she?"

"I don't know," he murmurs. "We don't know anything. Duke got her out of the building and they left in the ambulance while the crew was still working on the fire. We don't know what was wrong with her."

I practically drop my file on the floor. I barely keep my head enough to stuff it into the rack. "Where is she?! How far out are they?! I have to see her!"

"They're on their way in right now. I'll walk you down there."

I take off as fast as my bad leg will let me heading for the Emergency Department loading dock. Nothing better have happened to Oakleigh. I can't face that.

Keith stays by my side all the way there.

We only make it as far as the ED itself before the doors open from the loading dock.

The medical team and the paramedics surround the gurney in a cloud. Keith and I have to stand off to one side.

It takes a minute to figure out what the hell is going on. Drew and Allison wheel out the gurney with Oakleigh lying on it.

Everyone talks at once. The medical team tries to take Sophie's report at the same time other people are trying to talk to Duke.

He walks next to the gurney. He has his shirt off, but bandages cover most of his chiseled torso.

"You have to let go of her hand now, Chief," one of the nurses tells him. "We have to take her up to Radiology."

"I know that," he tells her and turns back to Oakleigh. "The medics are gonna take you inside, sweetie....."

She dives for his hand and practically throws herself off the gurney trying to get to him. "Don't leave me, Duke! Don't let go of me!"

"I'm right here, baby...." He tells her, but the same combination of nurses and medics won't let him get a word out.

"We need you to sit down on the gurney so we can take you into a trauma room...." one of the ED techs tells him.

"I don't need a gurney," he snarls. "You can see that I'm perfectly ambulatory." He tries to turn back to Oakleigh. "You're gonna be just fine, sweetheart. You need an X-ray. That's all...."

"We need to suture these lacerations...." the nurse goes on.

"I know that," Duke growls under his breath. "Will you just give me two seconds, please? I'm not in any danger right now."

I stand back staring at him and Oakleigh. She won't let go of his hand no matter what.

He has to fight off the medical team so he can bend over and get in her face. He has to talk loudly to make himself heard over all the noise.

"You have to go to Radiology now, sweetie. I'll be right down the hall. Nothing is going to happen to you. You're safe now. See? Keith and Ellen are here. They'll go with you."

He grabs her by the back of the head, kisses her hair, and pulls his hand out of her grasp. "I'm right here. I'm not going anywhere."

The medical team takes advantage of that moment to push the gurney away. The medics and ED techs hustle Duke away in the opposite direction.

He catches my eye before he walks out of the room. "She's fine!" he yells over his shoulder. "She has a broken leg just below the knee—but she's fine other than that! She's gonna be okay!"

The doors close between us and I lose sight of him.

"I don't believe it!" Keith mutters. "Just when I thought the guy couldn't pull off another miracle, he goes and does something like this."

I throw up my hands and walk away. "I gotta go to Radiology and see if she's okay."

He doesn't ask if I want him to come with me. He follows me.

He stands in silence outside the room while Oakleigh is inside. I call my manager and let her know I won't be going back on my shift for the rest of the day.

The radiologist comes out in a few minutes. Keith and I crowd around. "What's happening?" I ask. "How does it look?"

"It's a clean break, but the alignment is still off. Chief Broebeck's handover report said she had good perfusion to her foot and she still does. We just called upstairs for an orthopedic consult, but they'll probably put the leg in traction to bring the bones back into alignment before they cast it."

The radiologist leaves and I sink into a chair, cover my face, and heave a shaky sigh. "I'm really not cut out to be a parent. My nerves can't handle it."

Keith chuckles, sits down next to me, and hugs me around the shoulders. "Welcome to the trenches, sister. Be grateful you missed out on the whole throwing-up-in-the-middle-of-the-night stage."

I snort. Did I just make a big mistake by agreeing to have a child with Duke? Am I really ready for this?

Duke is right. Neither of us is ready. Neither of us will ever be ready.

I've heard other parents say that no one is ever ready for the responsibility and stress of having kids. I just never knew it would be this nerve-racking.

Why is it so nerve-racking, anyway? Oakleigh has a broken leg and it isn't even that bad.

The orderlies bring her out on the gurney in a second. She's still wearing the makeshift splint she had on in the ambulance.

The two side support pieces look like broken-off wooden table legs. The ties binding the leg into position look suspiciously like the tattered, charred fragments of a Howe County Fire Department T-shirt.

Oakleigh is much calmer now than she was before. She actually smiles at me and Keith.

We follow her upstairs where the orderly parks her in one of the ward rooms to wait for the orthopedic specialist to take a look at her X-rays.

I wait for all the orderlies and nurses to move away from her bed. Then I step forward and take her hand. "I'm so glad you're okay, sweetheart." I hear my voice shaking. "I was scared out of my mind when Keith told me you were coming in the ambulance."

"What happened?" Keith asks. "Duke said something about a broken gas main under the school."

"I don't know about that," she replies. "I was in the bathroom and I thought an earthquake went off. I fell over and hurt my leg. I couldn't get up. I got stuck in there. Then Duke showed up." She bursts into a huge grin. "He was so nice! I didn't think he could be so nice."

"What did you think—that he would be mean to you when you were trapped in a burning building with a broken leg?!" Keith counters. "We've been telling you all this time that he's a good guy."

"He's the best!" she gushes. "He was a hero."

"What did he do?" I ask.

"He said we had to get out of the building right away because he said the smell of gas was everywhere. He couldn't take the time to take care of my leg, so he picked me up and carried me out of the bathroom. We were on our way to the office when the whole building exploded. We fell down and he pulled me into the staffroom. That's where he put this thing on." She waves at the splint. "He had to break the window and then he climbed out."

"The principal says he saved a teacher and a bunch of other kids before he went back inside for you," Keith adds.

"He's such a great guy!" Oakleigh exclaims again. "He was so nice in the building. He kept telling me over and over that he was going to get me out. I thought we would die, but he handled everything. He deserves a medal for that."

Keith snorts. "I might have to step in as Fire Chief to get him one."

I pass my hand across my eyes. "That's amazing!"

I don't know why I'm surprised. Everyone in the Fire Department already knows Duke Broebeck is a hero.

I feel myself shaking as much from worry about Oakleigh as about him. Is this what my life is back to—worrying about Duke the way I used to worry about John?

That is the life I seem to be signing up for. This seems to be what the universe has in mind for me.

The orthopedic team comes just then. They have to start an IV and load Oakleigh up with truckloads of morphine before they put her leg in traction.

She's completely zonked out by the time they finish.

"I gotta get back to the firehouse and see what's happening with the crew and the truck and everything," Keith tells me. "Are you gonna be okay here on your own? I know we said she would stay with me and Danny for the next two weeks, but maybe she should stay in her own house for a while until this heals up."

I nod. "I'll be fine. Thanks. I'll take it from here."

"Go see what's happening with Duke," he tells me. "And then call me and let me know how injured he is."

I nod. I'm not sure if I'm ready to face Duke at all after today.

Keith leaves and I approach Oakleigh's bed to take her hand again. She floats around in a fog. Her glassy eyes barely register that I'm here.

"Ellen...." she croaks.

"I'm right here, baby," I murmur. "I'm right here with you."

"You and Duke....you should get married....." Her words slur and then she repeats herself. "You and Duke....you should get married.... you should have kids.....He should be a dad......"

Those words send a torch of fire through my heart. Duke. Am I really going to have children with him?

Chapter 22: Duke

I groan when I raise my arms to pull on the clean Fire Department T-shirt that Josh brought for me to wear.

Stitches cover my chest, arms, and shoulders—and don't even get me started on the burns on my back.

My body doesn't want to cooperate, but at least the shirt covers most of the bandages once I get the shirt on and straightened out.

I give myself this one moment to moan and groan about my sad, sorry fate, but at least all the kids made it out. I can take a few weeks to heal up from this after the day I just had.

I see movement behind me and turn around expecting the nurses to bring me my discharge paperwork.

I freeze when I see Ellen standing there. She stares at me in shocked horror—and then her eyes snap down to my T-shirt. Was she standing there watching me put it on?

I deflect her reaction by trying to make a joke about it. "How's the rug rat?"

Ellen gulps. Maybe I shouldn't have said something so tactless when her stepdaughter is in the hospital with a broken leg.

Ellen clears her throat and steps into the room. Her voice trembles when she finally finds the words to speak at all. "She's....she's fine..... Thank you....I don't know what to say."

"Don't say anything. I was just doing my job."

"But you....you could have died......"

She falters over the words—and looks away as tears spring to her eyes.

I cross the room in a fraction of a second. I want to put my arms around her and shower her in kisses, but this isn't the right time or place to do all of that.

I satisfy myself just by combing one lock of her hair out of her face. She's beautiful.

"Hey!" I breathe. "I'm okay! What did you think—that I was going to let a bunch of kids die in a burning building? Hey! Look at me! Are you going to be okay with being involved with another firefighter?"

"I already am involved with another firefighter!" Tears streak down her cheeks. "I'm already involved with Keith and Danny and the whole crew—and now you...."

She breaks off again. She doesn't say the other part.

If we really did this, if we had children together and built a life together, she would worry about me. No one has to spell it out for me.

Being married to a firefighter is no picnic. No one knows that better than she does.

"I don't know how to thank you...." she stammers again.

I can't let her flounder like this. I put my arms around her and pull her against me.

"You don't have to thank me," I murmur in her ear. "I would do anything for you and Oakleigh. You know that. She's a sweet kid and she was so nice to me in the building. I really think she's coming around about me."

She snorts and twists herself out of my arms. She bows her head and brushes tears off her cheeks in front of me. "She just told me we should get married. She says we should have children together."

I blink at her. "She said that?"

"She was in a morphine coma...but yeah. She wouldn't stop talking about how great you are—I mean, she said it while she was fully conscious. She thinks you're the greatest now."

I burst out laughing in relief. "Phew! I was so worried she was going to be the one to drive me off with a shotgun."

Ellen starts to smirk and tries to bite it back. "Now she's the one pushing us together."

"Would that be so bad?" I lay my hand against her cheek and stare deep into those big black eyes.

Emotion overflows my heart when I look at her. She's beautiful in every possible way.

I get another flashback of her straddling me and riding me while she orgasms. That memory is only slightly better than the memory of her passing out in sex-drunk exhaustion in my arms afterward.

"I want all of that with you," I murmur. "I want to make you happy."

Her face spasms with so much buried emotion. Watching her makes me ache for her. "I want to make you happy, too," she chokes. "I just don't know if I'm enough....."

"You are," I breathe. "You're more than enough. You're the only thing I want right now."

I want to kiss her, but I can only pull her into a deep embrace.

She gives me hope. Life goes on. I don't want it to—and yet I do want it to because she'll be in it.

She makes me want to find out what happens next.

Loving Ellen doesn't dishonor Naomi, Amelia, and the baby at all.

I can actually celebrate their lives more fully now that I'm with Ellen. Naomi, Amelia, and the baby are still a part of our family. They'll still be happy with us.

In a way, their deaths didn't end anything. It certainly didn't end the love and happiness available to all of us.

Me being happy with Ellen makes the love and happiness stronger for all of us to share it together. I understand that now.

She pries herself out of my arms again. "I better go back up there," she mumbles. "I don't want her to wake up when I'm not there."

"Yeah, you should." I lean in and kiss her on the forehead. "Call me if you need anything, okay?"

She nods. "Okay. I will."

I really want to tell her I love her. I should say it right now, but it's a little early in the set for that.

I do love her, though. I've loved her since the very first day I met her. Everyone loves Ellen. What's not to love?

She's more than a friend, more than a confidante. She's more than an acquaintance and more than my predecessor's widow.

She's everything I want....but I already told her that.

I can only stand and simmer with all these feelings when I watch her walk out of the room.

I'll see her again. I'll hold her again. I'll kiss her and enjoy the pleasures of her body again.

This is just the beginning. I have to be patient instead of trying to rush things like an overexcited teenager.

I feel like an overexcited teenager, but I'm not. I'm a middle-aged Fire Chief.

Just in case I forgot that fact, I'm on my way out of the hospital when I get a text from Keith. *What's the status with you? The mainte-*

nance driver is having a canary about the truck. Do you want me to sign it off?

I'm on my way back to the firehouse now, I tell him. *I'll meet you there and deal with it.*

I hit send, and a minute later, he replies, *All good.*

I take a split second to make up my mind and send back one more text. *After I sign off on the truck, I need to see you and Danny in my office.*

He takes extra long before he replies, *All right.*

He doesn't ask the reason why. Does he already know?

I catch a cab back to the firehouse and find Keith, Danny, Caleb, Carter, Josh, and Billy all standing around the maintenance driver.

He's going into full-blown hysterics about taking the other truck back.

"You're already here!" he tells the crew. "You know the truck is good! Just sign it off so I can leave! Do you know how much trouble I'm going to be in with my supervisor?!"

I walk in on the other guys trying to reason with him. "Don't worry, man," I tell the driver. "I can sign it off now."

"Why couldn't one of them sign it off? I've been waiting for more than five hours."

"They couldn't sign it off because I'm the Fire Chief around here." I look around. "Where's your paperwork? It doesn't look to me like you're as ready as you say you are."

The other guys roll their eyes to Heaven while the driver shimmies upstairs to get his paperwork.

"Was there anything wrong with the truck?" I ask while he's gone.

"Besides that fact that it isn't our usual rescue truck?" Keith asks. "It was fine."

The guys stand around while I sign off on the paperwork. The driver practically breaks down in tears when he finally gets behind the wheel.

Keith moves the new replacement vehicle out of the way so the driver can leave in the old truck. Calm descends over the firehouse.

Keith gives me a side look. "You okay?"

"I'll make it."

"How's the rug rat?" he asks.

I burst out laughing. I shouldn't, but hearing someone else ask that makes me giddy. I guess I wasn't being crass and tactless after all.

I feel my cheeks burning. Can he see what it is I want to talk to him and Danny about?

"I don't know how she is," I reply. "Ellen is still with her at the hospital. You should text her and find out."

He arches his eyebrows. "Are you ready to go upstairs?"

I nod and gulp down nerves.

He waves to Danny and they go first. We go up to my office—like I'm going to the principal's office or something.

The two brothers enter first. I have trouble steadying my nerves when I shut the door behind me and face these two men.

They already said they approve of me. I just have to get the words out.

"What's going on?" Keith rumbles. "Is something wrong with Oakleigh?"

"No, not at all. I just wanted you two to hear it from me first....that Ellen and I are involved. We hung out....yesterday....after the barbecue."

They both blink at me and then Danny snorts with stifled laughter. "Are you serious?! That's great! I didn't think you would really go for it! This is great!" He claps me on the back and bursts out in full laughter. "This is outstanding! Congratulations!"

"I'm not saying it will come to anything...."

"Oh, who do you think you're fooling, man?! It will come to something. You're a straight shooter. You're exactly what she needs—and she's exactly what you need."

I choke on overwhelming emotion. "Thanks."

"Is that it?" Keith asks. "Is that what you brought us here to tell us?"

"Well....yeah," I counter. "I had to tell you. You guys are practically her brothers. I mean...you are her brothers. Who else would I tell?"

Danny turns away. "We told you before. You don't have to explain yourself to us. Just do you and it will work out." He snickers to himself. "This is gonna be great!"

He leaves me alone with Keith. He furrows his brow at me the way he usually does.

I think he's gonna say something bad about me getting involved with Ellen, but he only crushes my shoulder in a death grip. "You're gonna be just fine, man—both of you. You deserve each other. You were made for each other. I'm sure John and Naomi would both agree that you and Ellen belong together."

He walks out and leaves me with a lump in my throat.

I knew both he and Danny would be okay with me getting together with Ellen. I just didn't know their approval would mean so much to me.

Chapter 23: Ellen

I jump out of my skin when I hear a knock at the door. I start to stand up, but Danny holds out his hand. "Stay where you are," he tells me and gives me a stern look.

My heart is already pounding out of my chest. I squirm in my seat while Danny opens the door.

We're in my house, but I guess all the firehouse guys have decided to go over the top with this traditional men-guarding-the-womenfolk thing.

Danny opens the door. Duke waits outside on the porch. He's wearing a suit.

"Come on in," Danny tells him and moves out of the way.

"Hi, Duke!" Oakleigh calls from the living room couch.

He glances in at her and smiles when he sees her with her leg in a cast. "Hey, munchkin," he greets her. "How's the haps?"

"Good!" She grins at him. "Have fun on your date!"

I turn bright red and head for the door.

"Be home by dawn!" Danny calls after me. "I wouldn't want to call in the Search and Rescue team."

Oakleigh laughs. I pretend not to hear, especially when I see Duke standing outside.

He looks unbelievable in his suit. This is the first time I've ever seen him wearing one except for when he married Naomi.

He doesn't look like a firefighter or even a Fire Chief. He looks like some kind of billionaire stud off the cover of a magazine. He looks like he should be on a yacht or on Wall Street or somewhere in the halls of governmental power.

His eyes skim down to my dress. I'm wearing a close-fitting black minidress, but I have to wear flats because of my brace. It kind of spoils the look, but that's just the price of doing business in my life.

His eyes widen. "Wow," he breathes. "You look sensational."

I blush and look away. "Thanks. You look pretty outstanding yourself."

He holds out his hand and a curious light comes into his eyes. "Are you ready?"

I can't help but laugh. I'm really nervous and giddy. We're going out on a date!

"Yeah!" I gasp and take his hand.

Danny and Oakleigh both yell out, "Bye!" as I pull the door shut behind me. He's babysitting her at my house while her leg heals up.

Duke's hand sends a rush of warmth up my arm. My heart turns a somersault when I see him grinning at me on our way down the driveway toward his truck. He's as excited as I am.

He has to walk slower to keep pace with me, but he doesn't act like my brace makes me any less attractive. I actually feel like I am when he looks at me like that.

He opens the passenger door for me to get in and then shoots me another wild smirk when he gets behind the wheel.

"Where are we going?" I ask as he pulls out of the driveway.

"Just a little out of the way place I know." He blushes and glances at me once before he goes back to concentrating on the road.

"Is it a surprise?"

"Yes," he replies.

I don't know what to say. I was never big on surprises. I might be really overdressed for wherever it is he wants to take me.

Then again, he's wearing a power suit, so I guess I'm not over-dressed.

I get even more nervous on the way into town. I really wish he wouldn't spring things like this on me.

I'm dwelling so much on figuring out where we're going that I don't realize where we actually are going. He drives toward town and then turns off onto a side street.

I get really confused when he drives around a few different blocks and pulls into the driveway of a stately house surrounded by big, overhanging trees.

This house can't be more than a quarter of a mile from my house. We're still in the same neighborhood where all the firehouse families live near the school.

The overhanging trees and thick stucco garden wall surround the property to give it a very private, wooded air, but it's right in the middle of the neighborhood—or on the edge of the neighborhood.

He pulls into the driveway. His headlights shine on a large two-story villa with ivy crawling all over the front porch.

"What is this place?" I half-whisper.

"This is my new house," he tells me. "Do you like it?"

"Your......" I stare at him. "What?"

He blushes at me in the glowing dashboard lights. "I bought a house. I thought you might want to move in with me and raise a few kids here." He switches off the headlights and the light dies. "Come inside and take a look around."

He gets out. It's completely dark outside, but as soon as he gets out, a bright, golden light switches on above the porch.

He lets me out, takes my hand, and leads me toward the front door.

I can't stop staring at everything. I never would have believed a place like this could exist right around the corner from all the quarter-acre suburban lots I think make up this neighborhood.

The grounds around the house are lush without being overgrown. The same ivy covers the garden wall. The ivy-covered wall gives the property a big, almost forested atmosphere.

The overhanging trees add to the effect that we're miles away from anyone or anything who might know us. We're insulated here.

I can definitely see how this would be the perfect place to raise kids. It's secluded, quiet, protected, and yet within walking distance of the school and all our friends.

He doesn't use his key when he opens the door. It opens into a big hall. This house has an old, Victorian-style staircase rising to the second story. Carved wooden cornices and top plates surround every doorway and windowpane.

A long hall cuts through the house from front to back. The living room sits on one side with a really nice antique-style parlor across the hall.

Duke shoots me another blushing smirk. "Do you want to go inspect the upstairs bedrooms?"

"You actually bought this?!" I gasp. "You....you own this?!"

"Do you like it? I thought it would be the perfect place to have kids...."

"You're serious?!" I interrupt. "You're....."

I glance around as the truth sinks in. He's really serious about having kids—with me.

I get a blast of mental imagery about what living here with him and raising kids would be like. Any child who grew up here would lead a charmed life.

I used to think the neighborhood around the school was the best place kids could possibly grow up. They're surrounded by their friends and supportive, protective adults.

Now I'm seeing a whole new dimension of possibilities. I can't imagine anything better than this house.

Duke is more than serious. He's actually planning for it to happen. He doesn't even let himself think it wouldn't happen. He already bought the flippin' house.

He takes my hand. "You don't have to decide right now," he murmurs. "Come here. I have something for you."

He leads me down the hall. We pass an enormous farmhouse kitchen on the left and an actual wood-paneled library on the right.

I might be mistaken, but I think I spot some of the same books in there that I packed up from Naomi's old house. Duke didn't get rid of his stuff after all.

Did he keep all of Amelia's baby gear, too? Is he planning as far ahead as that?

I don't know what to think, but my heart stops all over again when he turns into a big, fancy dining room also paneled in dark wood. The place smells like a museum, but I don't see a single speck of dust anywhere.

A large candelabra burns on the big carved table. Ten candles brighten the room.

He leads me to the other end of the table where he's set two places for an exquisite, restaurant-quality dinner. He even has dishes covered in silver domes waiting for us.

He pulls out my chair for me to sit down. "Madam....."

I snort with laughter. "Is that what you're going to start calling me?"

He smirks again. "Only if you misbehave."

He pushes my chair in, sits down in his own seat at an angle to me, and opens a bottle of wine—or rather, he picks up a bottle of wine that is already open.

I take in the whole scene in a heartbeat. He must have set all of this up ahead of time.

He set the table, cleaned the house to a spotless shine, and even opened the wine.

He pours me a glass and takes the covers off the dishes. Steam billows from underneath and the savory smell of spicy meat fills the room.

He keeps blushing and smiling at me on the side. "I thought we would take a break from Mexican."

Chapter 24: Ellen

D uke serves me a big helping of stuffed cannelloni dripping with cheese and sauce.

He holds out his hand to me and we hold hands while we eat.

"This is a really good restaurant," I tell him. "I'm going to have to recommend this one to all my friends."

He snorts with laughter. "Don't. I already have a job."

"These cannelloni are fantastic. How did you get to be such a good cook?"

"A single guy cooking for himself gets pretty boring after a while if he doesn't learn how to make it more interesting."

I study him across the table. "You might wind up cooking for the family if you can pull off something like this."

He turns bright red and pushes his food around on his plate. "I would love to."

I watch him eat and get the sense again of what an amazing treasure he is. The universe certainly gave him a few strikes, but none of that mars his pure character.

He's an amazing man. Any woman would be lucky to get together with him—and any child would be lucky to have him as a father.

I get another mental flash of how he used to act around Amelia. The fates sure did smile on her when her mother gave Amelia to Duke instead of someone else.

A million ideas flood my mind when I look around this house. Any child would be lucky to grow up here....with us.

Would a child be that lucky to grow up with me as its mother? He certainly seems to think so.

Oakleigh and the Brewer boys think so, too. Who am I to argue with them? No one understands family better than they do.

We finish eating and Duke leans back in his chair swirling his wine glass. "So how is Oakleigh doing?"

"She's great. She's in a much better mood since she broke her leg."

He laughs. "I wasn't trying to imply anything."

"Oh, I think you had plenty to do with it."

"Me?!" His hand flies to his heart in mock horror. "I had nothing to do with it."

"It really made me wonder if maybe she never had a problem with you and me at all. Maybe it was just you—like maybe she resented the fact that you came to work here and took over for her dad. Maybe the simple fact that anyone had to take over for her dad rubbed her wrong. I don't know. It's just a thought. I only know her attitude has done a complete U-turn. She's back to being chipper and delightful the way she was before John died."

"Do you really think I made that much difference to her?"

"She was able to see that you really are a good guy. She doesn't have any reason to hate you anymore. Okay, so you aren't her dad, but that isn't your fault."

"How do you think she would deal with...." He waves around him. "With all of this?"

"I don't know, but it seems like the fire gave her the opening she needs to finally put the past behind her. Maybe she realizes she doesn't have to hold onto it anymore—kind of like we're doing."

He looks down at his wine in his glass. "I'm glad you see it that way. I'm glad you don't think I'm being heartless by moving on right away."

"Not at all. You aren't getting any younger. If you want to have a family, why not start now?"

He looks up at me and his eyes harden. "Tell me the truth about what you think of the house."

My jaw drops. "The house?! You really think I would have a problem with the house?! Are you crazy?"

"I wasn't sure if it was too much."

"Too much?!" I practically shriek. "It's magnificent!"

"So does that mean it's too much?"

"NO!!" I counter. "It's perfect!"

"Because I want it to be comfortable."

"It is! It's wonderful."

"I want you to be comfortable here, too. I don't want you to feel out of place or...."

"Will you stop that?!" I roar. "The house is wonderful. It's sublime. It's perfect. It's stupendous."

He snorts again. "Stupendous? I don't want it to be stupendous."

"You know what I mean. Besides.....how many kids are you planning for us to have?"

He laughs again. "How much time do we have left?"

I blush and look away. He takes the opportunity to stand up and lift my hand off the table. "Come with me."

I stand up. He pulls out my chair and waits while I lock my knee joint.

He leads me up the stairs and down a long, carpeted hall. It's dark in here, but golden lamplight glows from the bedroom at the far end of the upstairs landing.

A big, curved bay window looks out over the shadowy grounds. I can just imagine the view of the property from up here.

He turns into what has to be the master bedroom. It's a giant room with a huge sleigh bed and heavy, solid, carved antique furniture all around the room.

A bench seat nestles under another bay window looking away from the street. That must be a really nice place to sit and relax.

Duke drifts into the room behind me. It couldn't be more obvious why he brought me here. He wants this to be our room.

He eases toward me. I get one look at his eyes before he scoops me up behind my back in both arms and lifts me to his height to kiss me.

What is he going to do this time? Is he going to pin me against the wall....or something else?

He backs toward the bed, pulls my legs around him, and sits down. I have to quickly unlock my knee so I can straddle him.

"Spend the night with me," he murmurs into my mouth. "Let's pretend—just for tonight."

I lean back to study him from only a few inches away. "Pretend? Aren't we already doing this?"

His eyebrows shoot up. "Are we?"

"We already did it when I'm not on any birth control. Me spending the night with you tonight would only be further confirmation that we're doing it. What am I missing?"

He smiles at me. "Nothing, I guess."

"Are we doing this?" I ask. "Isn't this what you want?"

"Yes. I wouldn't have asked you if I didn't."

I study him. He doesn't seem to be doing anything.

We sit here in the glowing lamplight. We're both dressed up to the nines, but this doesn't feel like a fancy date.

He's right. We're home. We aren't pretending. It's just happening.

He shifts me off his lap and sits me down on the bed. "I'm going to go downstairs, blow out the candles, and turn off the lights. I'll be right back." He heads for the door.

"Do the dishes while you're up!" I call after him.

His laughter vanishes down the stairs.

I glance around the room. This is the nicest bedroom I can ever remember being in. It's even nicer than some hotel rooms I've seen.

I sit there trying to decide what to do. He could come back at any minute.

Should I act all sexy so he gets a nice surprise when he comes back?

I make up my mind, shimmy out of my dress, bra, and panties, kick off my shoes, and take off my brace.

I dive under the covers stark naked and pull them up to my chin. He can't see any part of me below the neck.

My heart races waiting for him to come back upstairs. He said he wanted to pretend we're already married, living here, and raising a family.

I wouldn't hesitate to get into bed if we were. I might be wearing pajamas...or I might not.

I catch my breath when I hear him climbing the stairs. Will that sound become familiar in the years ahead? Will I be able to track his movements through the house by sound alone?

This must be how mothers become innate lie detectors for their kids' misbehavior. The mothers become hyper-tuned to every sound that happens in their houses even when it happens at a distance.

Duke comes back into the room. His eyes go hard again when he sees me lying in bed—our bed. He wants this to be our bed.

He shuts the bedroom door with a kind of finality that rings through the eons. It's over. It's done. The decision has been made—somewhere.

He starts taking off his suit. He doesn't face me when he does it. He isn't performing a strip tease here. We're at home alone in our bedroom about to go to bed for the night.

He crosses to the large carved oaken wardrobe standing against the far wall, opens it, and starts hanging his suit on a hanger along with all his other clothes.

His uniforms hang in there, too. His boots and casual sneakers rest on the bottom floor of the wardrobe. He really does live here. This is his house.

He drapes his tie over the hanger rail, strips off his shirt, hangs it up, and kicks off his shoes and socks.

He puts his shoes back inside the wardrobe and tosses his socks into a laundry hamper in the corner.

He shucks off his pants and leaves his shorts on. He goes through every step of the process with casual methodical indifference—like he does this every day.

He crosses to the bed and smiles at me for the first time when he draws the covers down to get in. He pushes his shorts off as he sits down, switches off the light, and slides in next to me.

He pulls the covers over both of us and our heat joins into a seamless river of blissful silky softness.

Moonlight winks beyond the trees and shines through the window. The moon casts a ghostly silver sheen over the bed with us in it.

Duke lets out a shaky breath and turns toward me. I expect him to kiss me. The moon reflects in his eyes.

His cheekbones and forehead glisten with a different kind of light. His weight rolling on top of me feels like it has been coming since the dawn of time.

I stroke his cheeks as he hovers there above me. His eyes drill into my soul. His body doesn't come to life to take me. He just stays there, together with me for all time.

"I love you," he whispers.

"I love you, too," I whisper back. Those words mean so much and yet they don't even begin to describe what I see in him right now.

My fingertips trace the timeless beauty of his angelic face. This is the man I'm going to spend the rest of my life with. This is the man who will be the father of my children.

From an impossible distance, he twists his hips between my legs and pushes my thighs apart. His hardness slides into me on a film of the same glistening diamond light....and still his eyes never leave me for a second.

He watches all that light and meaning radiating out of my eyes and back to him. He sees me as I am—in the fullness of what I can be and will become in the halo of his love.

His body contracts on top of me to drive his shaft deep inside me. He'll plant his seed in me—right here in the bed that will be our marriage bed for all time.

Our children will cuddle up in this bed. They'll sleep with us when they get sick. They'll run in here and jump up and down on us when we want to sleep in on Sunday morning.

My mother's intuition will make me watch our children from that bay window while they play outside. They'll wonder how I found out what they were doing when I wasn't there.

I should laugh or at least smile at all those pictures coming into my head.

I can't laugh or even smile. They all seem so inevitable and timeless. They're already happening and already have happened.

Chapter 25: Duke

Sophie sticks her head through my office door. "Duke! We're heading over to the beach! Come on! It's barbecue time!"

"I'm coming!" I call after her. "I'm right behind you. Just let me save this...."

"You're such a nerd!" she yells from down the hall. The crew is already crowding into the garage to leave for the barbecue.

I don't let myself think about the fact that I'll see Ellen there. Things have been going so fast between us....and this morning she just told me she's pregnant. I can't wait!

We haven't told everyone yet. We haven't told anyone. I'm not sure I can.

She's been staying with Oakleigh at her house until Oakleigh gets her leg out of her cast. We plan to hold off until then before Ellen and Oakleigh move into my house—our house.

Ellen thinks we might still have to stay at John's old house on the weeks when Ellen takes care of Oakleigh—just to give Oakleigh a sense of continuity.

I don't care about that as long as we're working toward our future together.

I close all the documents I have open on my computer, straighten my stack of applicant resumes, and stand up to leave my office.

I freeze when Vince Jaeger walks through the door. He's barely said a word to me since the whole Ellen disaster.

He's been keeping his nose clean, but he gets a lot of help from the Brewers—maybe a little too much help.

This must be serious if he's cornering me in my office alone. Today is his day off. He shows up in his casual clothes.

He actually looks like he's ready to go out to the beach to meet the crew.

"What's up?" I ask as calmly as I can. "Aren't you going to the barbecue?"

He takes a deep breath and his lips shiver. He actually looks like he's about to cry. "I'm here to resign from the firehouse."

My jaw drops. "What?! Why?! You've been doing great! Why would you leave? You're kicking ass on this crew. You can't leave!"

He looks down at his hands like he doesn't recognize them. "I can't stand to see you and Ellen together. You got her. I really thought I had a chance after John died.....She kept saying she wasn't ready....but she actually meant she wasn't ready for me. She was ready for you, though. I can't stay here. I have to move away—to another town—maybe the other side of the country."

My shoulders slump. "I'm sorry, man. I never meant to cut you out."

He shrugs at nothing. "I guess it makes sense—both of you losing someone like that. She was never gonna pick me. I'm not you."

I don't know what to say. "Do you really have to quit...because of this?"

"I have to," he husks. "I don't want to, but working here.....Every one supports you. None of them will ever let me forget it....and now I can't even be around her. I couldn't go to the barbecues....and what am I even doing here if I'm not part of the family?"

"I'm sorry, man," I exclaim. "I had no idea this would happen."

He finally raises his eyes to meet mine. "I don't blame you. I really don't. You're one lucky bastard, you know that?"

"I know," I choke. "I know."

"Just give me a good reference, okay? Don't leave me hanging. Let me start over somewhere else—somewhere I might be able to find a place."

"I will! You're an outstanding firefighter. I hate to lose you."

He shrugs and lowers his eyes again. "I'm gonna get out of here. Maybe you can explain everything to people at the barbecue so I don't have to face them."

"Sure, man. Anything you want—and don't worry about the reference. I won't be able to recommend you highly enough. Let me know if you need me to write you a letter or anything like that."

"Okay. See you."

He walks out. I can only stand and stare as his footsteps fade down the stairs. That's the last time. He won't come back.

Poor guy. I sure wish he wouldn't quit, but I can't say I blame him.

I'll have to explain this to Ellen. I don't think she realizes how deep his feelings for her were.

It didn't sound like he made it clear to her. I got the impression that he was trying to keep it light, friendly, and casual. He probably didn't communicate to her that he wanted something serious.

Then again, she's probably out of his league after being married to a man like John Brewer. I never met the guy, but his legacy speaks for itself.

She worked with Vince for years before she got together with John. She's already told me she had a crush on him all that time and never said anything.

She would have gotten together with Vince a long time ago if it was going to happen at all.

She also told me about her conversation with Danny. He says she only likes the best and he's right. She has high-class taste in men.

If she set her heart on the Fire Chief, she wouldn't likely settle for a run-of-the-mill firefighter just because the Fire Chief was a single father, her boss, and completely off the market after his previous wife's death.

She never looked sideways at Vince or any of the other firehouse guys. She loved John. She didn't want anyone else.

I love that about her, but I still feel sorry for Vince. He just wasn't the man for her.

No sound comes from the garage anymore. I'm the only person left in the firehouse. I better go while the getting is good.

I head out to my pickup and drive to the beach. Everyone else is already here—except for Vince, of course.

I get there and spot Ellen lifting a shopping bag out of her trunk. It's the bag of water guns I bought for the kids to play with last time.

I park next to her. She waits for me to get out. "Hey!" She beams when she greets me. "I was wondering when you were gonna show up."

I ease over to her, put my arms around her, and kiss her. "I have to tell you something."

Her head shoots up. "Is it something bad?"

"Not bad on the firehouse scale, but it isn't good. Vince just quit. He's leaving town. He said he can't stand to see us together."

Her face falls. "Oh, that's terrible! Isn't there any way to talk him out of it?"

"I don't think so. I tried. His mind is already made up. He asked me to pass the word to the crew so he doesn't have to. I thought you should hear it first."

She looks away and blinks into empty space. "Oh. I didn't know he felt that way about me."

"You didn't know probably because you never felt that way about him. You told him you weren't ready, but what you actually meant was that you weren't ready for him. You were ready for me."

She looks up. "Do you really think so?"

"That's what he said....and it makes sense, doesn't it? You didn't have a problem getting together with me even when you said you weren't ready. If it was meant to be between you and Vince, you would have even if you weren't ready."

"I guess so."

I squeeze her hand. "Take a walk with me. I'm not ready to share you with everyone else yet."

She grins, puts the bag of water guns on the ground by her car, and slips her hand into mine. I don't want to lead her onto the same stretch of beach where I had my first date with Naomi. That would be crude.

I lead her around on the road to the park adjacent to the beach. We walk through the trees and rose gardens.

"What did you want to talk to me about?" she asks.

I turn to face her and squeeze her hands. "Marry me. I don't want to wait anymore. I don't want to announce it to the crew that you're pregnant when we don't have a plan in mind to get married."

She blinks up at me with those big dark eyes of hers. *"Do* we have a plan in mind for getting married?"

I shrug that away. "How about the next barbecue? We can do it here."

Her eyes fall out of their sockets. "The next barbecue?! That's in two weeks, Duke!"

"I know when it is. We can keep it low-key. All our friends and family will already be here. Everybody else always has firehouse weddings. I don't want to do the same thing as everyone else."

"But....don't you think two weeks from now is a little sudden? We're barely dating....I mean, it's two weeks from now! That doesn't give us much time to plan anything."

"When would you like to do it?"

"I don't know! Maybe a month at least....or two months."

I find myself beaming at her. "So does that mean yes?"

Her head shoots up at me. "Yes what?"

"Will you marry me?"

"Of course! You know I will! You shouldn't even have to ask that!"

"Well, I do have to ask it. I haven't asked you before."

"I thought we already were."

"When did you think we were?"

She blinks at me. "Um....I didn't really think about that."

I laugh at her. Then I pull the ring box out of my pocket and crack it open in front of her eyes.

She stares at the ring with her mouth open. She's still staring at it in blank disbelief when I pull the ring out and slip it on her finger.

She stands there staring at it with the same stunned expression even after I put it on her hand and let go.

I wait, but I don't get any response. "Ellen? Are you okay with this?"

She bursts to life so suddenly that she startles me into jumping back. She spins away and chops her hand through the air—the hand with the ring on it. "Oh, we are so getting married! Come on! We have to get back to the barbecue and tell everyone."

I chuckle to myself on our way back to the beach. She has to stop herself and slow down to walk next to me.

She comes back to her senses and smiles at me when she takes my hand. I smile back. It's all on. Now we just have to make our announcements to the crew.

We get back to the beach to find everyone in their usual places—except one person.

Brooke frowns at the surroundings. "Where's Vince? He saw him stop by the firehouse. He should have gotten here by now."

"He isn't coming," I blurt out. "He quit the crew this morning."

Everyone spins around to gasp and gape at me. "He what?!" they all bellow.

I go through the whole explanation all over again. "And now Ellen and I are getting married," I announce. "So he definitely wouldn't want to stick around for that."

"You're....you're getting married.....so soon?" Emily stammers. "But you guys have only been dating for...like....."

"And Ellen is pregnant," I go on. "So we have to. I mean...we don't *have* to, but we want to....so we are." I turn to Ellen. "Is it the next one or the one after that?"

She turns bright red and her eyelashes dip. God, she turns me on! "Let's call it six weeks. That's enough time, isn't it?"

"Six weeks?!" Jessie blurts out. "You're getting married in six weeks?!"

"Duke wanted to do it at the next barbecue," Ellen tells her. "So count yourselves lucky."

"We can do it," I tell them. "We're going to have it here—so it will be on one of our barbecue Saturdays. We're going to keep it casual and understated."

"You can't do that!" Leila gasps. "What about the chairs.....and the arch....and the music....and the caterers....."

"Forget all that. We don't need all that. We can just do it like this." I turn to Ellen and take both her hands. "Ellen Foreman, I, Duke Broebeck, do hereby promise to love, honor, and cherish you, for better or for worse....."

"Stop!!" Leila shrieks so loudly that she makes Leon start crying. "You can't say the vows now! You aren't getting married now!"

"I'm just proving my point. We already have enough food. We don't need chairs because we're all standing around anyway. We don't need an arch. We just need me, Ellen, all of you, and the vows."

"But....who will marry you?" Sophie asks. "You usually officiate weddings."

"Keith married me and Naomi....."

"But he can't marry us," Ellen cuts in. "Keith has to walk me down the aisle....I mean the sand."

Laughter starts to break out.

"I'll marry you," Danny interjects. "To hell with it. I might as well."

Excited talk breaks out. The men and women split up and start talking in rapid streams of dialogue on both sides.

Ellen gets swept over to the women's side. I watch from afar. I'm sure I'll get roped into this sooner rather than later, but I don't care.

It's happening, and once it does, there will be no stopping us from making all our dreams come true.

The End.

Get All of AE Moran's Free Books

S ign Up Once—Get all A.E. Moran's free books including brand
new releases

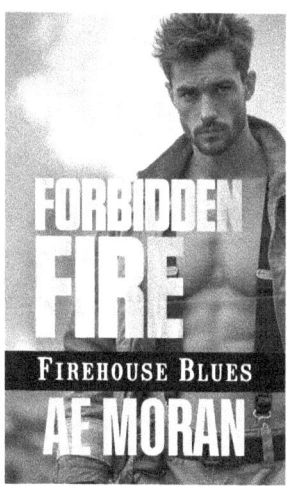

When what you want most is the one thing you can never have......

Austin McAuliffe is every woman's dream firefighter—young, strong, drop-dead hot, and selflessly dedicated to his career—and to the woman of his heart, Emma Brady. Only one other person holds a place in Austin's life—his best friend and fellow firefighter, Theo Gough. Austin insists on Theo spending time with Austin and Emma as a couple, especially when these two firefighters have a hard day at the office.

No one can believe when Austin completely flips out and randomly accuses Theo and Emma of flirting with each other in front of the whole fire crew. Could there be some deeper, more sinister reason for Austin to suddenly lose his mind and lash out at those closest to him?

Emma is devastated when Austin coldly dumps her with no warning and disappears out of her life, but Austin casts a long shadow. The nightmare of his sudden betrayal will come back to haunt Emma and Theo long after Austin is gone. Will the ghosts of the past ruin any chance for them to regain their happiness.....or will Austin's madness take down everyone he cares about along with him?

Sign up at www.authoraemoran.com to read it for free.

About AE Moran

A.E Moran is the contemporary romance pen name for Theo Mann.

I write 70 books per year—and yes, before you ask, all these books are my original creative work. Nothing written under my name is AI-generated or ghostwritten because I write better than AI and any ghostwriter out there.

People don't read fiction for entertainment or to escape from reality. People read fiction to see their humanity reflected in another person's character and story.

This is my promise to you. When you read my books, you'll see your own humanity reflected in the characters and stories. I take this commitment to my readers very seriously. My books are an intimate form of communication between us. I would never disrespect my readers by turning that over to a machine or another writer. This is my bond between me and you as my reader.

I write 20,000 words per day as my daily work output. If anyone with a public platform would like to challenge me to prove this in a controlled environment, feel free to contact me on this website's contact page.

I worked as a professional ghostwriter for fifteen years. Now I'm going for the Guinness World Record by writing 700 books over the next ten years and 1400 books over the next twenty years, all originally written by me. See my website for the full book list.

I'm also the author of *Proof for the Existence of God* and the *Crimes Against Fiction* blog. You can find all my nonfiction work at www.crimes-against-fiction.com.

If you have a story idea, or if you would like me to explore a series in more depth, or if you'd like me to explore a character by writing a spinoff series about that character or world, leave me a message on my website's contact page. I answer all reader emails, so ask me anything, tell me what you liked and didn't like, and let me know where you'd like your favorite series to go. I would love to hear your ideas and find out what you'd like to read next.

You can find out more at www.theomann.com or at www.authoraemoran.com.

Also by AE Moran (so far)

www.ingramcontent.com/pod-product-compliance
Lightning Source LLC
Chambersburg PA
CBHW051651260626
47170CB00004B/1438

* 9 7 8 1 9 9 1 4 0 0 5 8 1 *